# DEAD RIVER

# ALSO BY BILL LIGHTLE

(Non-Fiction)

*Made or Broken:*
*Football & Survival in the Georgia Woods*

*Mill Daddy:*
*The Life & Times of Roy Davis*

*My Mother's Dream:*
*Baseball with the Bankers*

*To Dance with the Devil's Daughter:*
*God's Restoration of the Rev. Grady Caldwell*

*Don't Tell Your Mother:*
*My Adventures with the Kevin Simpkins Gang*

# DEAD RIVER

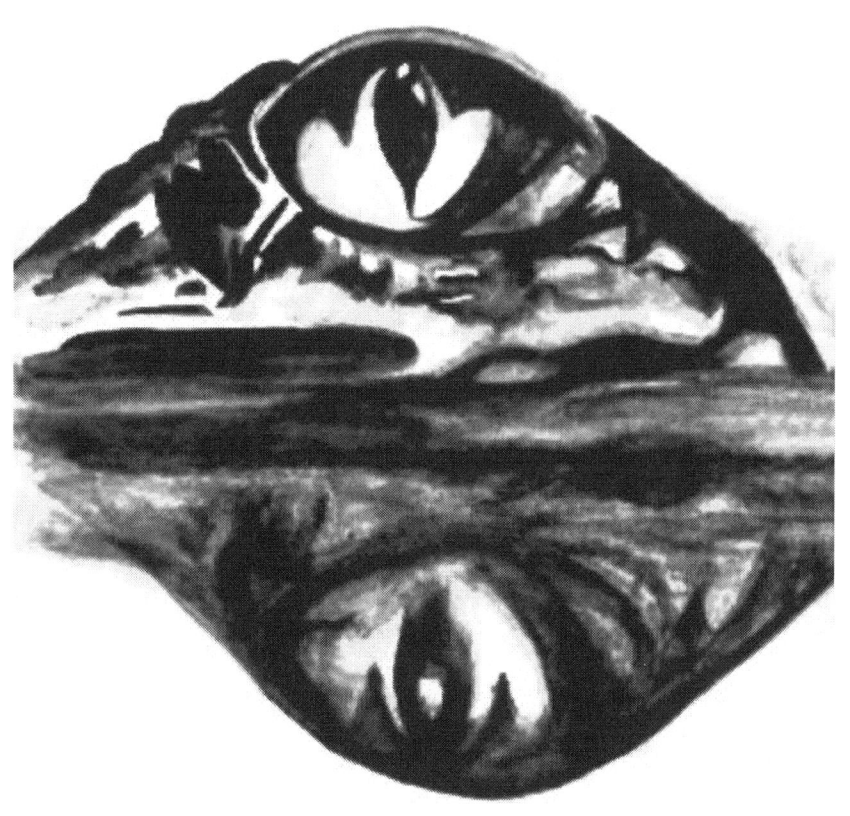

## BILL LIGHTLE

DEAD RIVER
Copyright © 2015 Bill Lightle

Cover Art by Anna Cone

Printed and bound in the United States of America. All rights reserved. No part of this book may be reproduced in any form or by any electronic or mechanical means, including information storage and retrieval system, without permission in writing from the copyright holder, except by reviewer, who may quote brief passages in review.

ISBN: 978-1517015725
Published by Bill Lightle
285 Kari Glen Drive
Fayetteville, GA 30215
229-881-5872

This is a work of fiction based on actual events in South Georgia in the early 1980s.

For Phyllis

*…That every year I have cried, 'At length
My darling understands it all,
Because I have come into my strength,
And words obey my call…'*
                                        W. B. Yeats

# CHAPTER 1

I had just finished a story on the county commissioners' meeting when I heard, over the hymns from the typewriters, the unmistakable voice from the back of the newsroom.

"Maynard, Maynard. I need you over here. Now. Right now."

I walked to where the voice had come from and stood in front of Mickey Burke, executive editor of the *Albany Chronicle*. He was at his desk and from it every reporter in the newsroom was in full view. A dozen black Royal manual typewriters sounded as if they were conducted by a famed choirmaster. Mickey was the consummate choirmaster.

"What is it, Mickey? What you got for me?"

"I just got a call from someone on the Flint River. He said a company up there is polluting the river. Said the river's turning black. The guy was raising hell. Said there are dead fish everywhere. I want you to check it out and see if there's a story there. I need it done. You understand?"

Mickey took a drink of coffee then a long pull from a cigarette. I was about to ask a question, but he spoke again machine-gun style. The same way he always did. Coffee and cigarettes he consumed as if they were life-sustaining. I believed they were for him.

"He says there's something black covering the river. Here's his name and phone number. I want you to call him and let me know what he says. Let's move on this goddamnit. It could be something big. Let's find out. You never know goddamnit. Here."

Mickey handed me a piece of thin tan typing paper with a name and telephone number written on it in pencil. The writing was sloppy, but I could read it well.

Mickey's "goddamns" were as common as quotation marks in a news story. They didn't seem like cussing after my first week on the job. That was just Mickey. If he spoke, he cussed. For weeks after I started working under him, his profanity and the often wild-eyed excitement he got over a news story intimidated me. Equal amounts of blood and newspaper ink ran through his veins, I thought. In the beginning it was difficult for me to relax around him. With time that changed, but he didn't change. If you did your job faithfully, asked good questions, got good quotes, he'd praise you. If you paid attention, you could learn a lot from him. I understood all of this in the beginning.

"Okay, Mickey. I'll call the guy right now. I'll take care of it. I got it."

I took the paper from Mickey and walked to my desk and sat down in a black leather chair on wheels. The desk had two big drawers on both sides and contained typing paper, reporter notepads, phone books, and pens. I picked up the telephone and dialed. After the second ring someone picked up.

"Hello."

"Hello, I'm John Maynard with the *Albany Chronicle,* and I want to speak with Tony Patrick."

"That would be me. I'm Tony Patrick. Yeah, buddyro. I called your paper because I'm pissed off up here about what's happenin' to our river. What these assholes have done to it. It's a damn black mess. They're killin' this river. That's what those assholes are doin'. They're just killin' it. I've never seen anything like it, and if you get up here you'll say the same. I promise you that."

"What assholes?"

"The ones that are killin' everything on our river. Those assholes."

"Who's killing who?"

"No, nobody's dead, not yet anyway. Fish, turtles, ducks that's what I'm talkin' about. I saw a dead alligator yesterday. They're hard to kill. They've been around millions of years and God Almighty they're beautiful animals. Just beautiful. Those company sumbitches. They're all sumbitches. All of 'em."

I didn't know what company the man who loved alligators was

referring to. I waited five seconds hoping he would take a long, deep breath. I needed a rest and so did my source on the other end of the line, I thought. Tony Patrick's cussing and sharp sentences reminded me of how Mickey spoke in the newsroom. It was familiar music.

"Mr. Patrick, can you tell me what's going on up there? What's happening on the Flint?"

"I can tell you all about it, but I need to show you. You need to see this. Someone needs to see this shit that's happenin' to our river. Hell, everyone needs to see what's happenin' here. Come up here, and I'll show you. I'll show you everything."

"I do want to know more about what's happening up there. That's why I called. What can you tell me?"

"I'll tell you what's happenin', these folks are killin' a damn fine river. You come up here, and I'll take you on a boat ride right past the company. You won't believe this shit. Come see for yourself. I was raised on this river, and now it's a damn mess."

"Mr. Patrick, what company are you talking about?"

"Hell, everybody knows. It's Transpower Inc. Or *Transcrewed.*"

I knew the company, Transpower Inc., had built a plant on the Flint River near Cordele, Georgia, about forty miles from Albany, and had begun production a few months earlier. It made paper products. Paper towels, disposable diapers, and toilet paper. It was the company's first plant in Georgia, getting an abundant supply of pine trees and water from the Flint River. That's why it was there.

Another reporter from the paper had attended the opening-day company celebration that included the governor and one of the state's senators. I couldn't remember which one. It was a big deal. Speeches had been given about the goodness of the men who ran the multi-million dollar corporation, and the five hundred high-paying jobs that Transpower had brought to Georgia. They promised more jobs would come. I had read all of the story. I remembered talking to David Price who covered it for the *Chronicle*, and he said there had been a tour of the plant and plenty of food for the media and gift baskets full of the products that the plant would make. "It was some public relations show," David said.

"When would you like for me to come up, Mr. Patrick?" I said.

"Right now. Come up this afternoon and I'll show you what I been talkin' about."

"All right. Let me talk to my editor. Why don't you go ahead and give me directions to your house." Tony Patrick gave me directions, and I wrote them on my notepad.

"What time will you be here?"

"I'll be there in about an hour. If for some reason my editor has something else for me, I'll call you right back. But I'm almost certain he wants me to come up there today."

"Okay buddyro, I'll see you then."

I hung up the telephone and walked back to Mickey's desk. Mickey had graduated from the University of Georgia with a degree in journalism and later became an officer in the Green Berets and served two tours of duty in Vietnam before returning to Albany to begin work on the paper. His dad owned the *Chronicle*. Mickey kept pictures of his Vietnam war buddies and large killing knives hung on the wall behind his desk. He carried those knives in Vietnam and talked about the ways he used them against the North Vietnamese. He loved telling these stories and could scare the hell out of you.

Mickey was a good editor, and the only one I had known, having been hired by him a few years earlier at twenty-three. I had graduated from Georgia Southwestern College in nearby Americus in 1980, and a few weeks later was working for the *Chronicle*.

"Well, Maynard what the hell did that man say?"

He took a pull from a Marlboro. Smoke engulfed the newsroom. It was as constant as the humming of the big presses that printed each morning. The other editors and most of the reporters smoked the same incessant way. I didn't smoke, but inhaled enough from others that I sometimes coughed the same way they did. He was on his second pack of the day. He flipped his ashes in a saucer-size, large glass ashtray that was inscribed: "Mekong Delta – Let the Killing Begin."

"I told him I'd come see him and the river this afternoon. He says there's dead fish everywhere. The guy was really hot. It sounds like it might be a story, Mickey. I want to go up there if I can."

Mickey nodded in the direction of the front door of the newsroom.

"Go. Get some good quotes, write down everything you see and tell me about it first thing in the morning. If there's something there goddamnit, I want to know. Got it?"

"Okay, Mickey. I'll see you in the morning. I got it."

I walked back to my desk and took two notepads from a desk drawer, two fresh black pens, an expense sheet for mileage and left the newsroom. I thought about taking my camera, then decided against it. Mickey didn't mention sending a photographer with me, and I usually only took pictures if there wasn't one available. "Don't give me some damn Mexican execution, Maynard, when you take a picture," Mickey said, the few times I did take pictures for a news story. "Now goddamnit, don't forget that. No damn Mexican execution." It didn't take me long to figure out that he meant the people in the photos I took looked like they were facing a firing squad.

If this turned out to be something good, Mickey would send one of the three photographers to the river with me, I thought. He would want plenty of art if the story played out.

I walked out of the office and took off my tie on the way to my car and opened the door to the 1976 brown LTD Ford. For the last three weeks the air conditioning had been blowing air that wasn't even cool. Now I wished again I had gotten it fixed.

"Damn this heat!"

I started my car and pulled away from the office, driving west on Pine Avenue. I could damn the heat all I wanted, but words weren't going to make it go away. It was South Georgia. It was July. I put in an eight-track tape of Bob Dylan and The Band, *Before the Flood,* and turned it up loud and rolled down the driver's window, and the words filtered out. "The Night They Drove Old Dixie Down." Lyrics and music kept my mind off the heat for a while, but not long.

I begin to think about the river and Tony Patrick as I drove away from the newsroom and through downtown Albany toward my house on North Cleveland, five minutes from the newsroom. In high school and college, I had spent many days on the Flint boating and tubing with friends. The riverbanks were lined with cypress trees and occasional sandy beaches. Good times and good memories on a beautiful stretch of water.

I pulled into the driveway of my house that I rented with a friend and got out and went inside. My roommate was at work teaching writing classes at Albany Junior College. I took off my office clothes and put on shorts, tennis shoes, a Panama City Beach T-shirt, and a baseball cap and left. I was headed to the Flint. I was ready for a boat ride.

# CHAPTER 2

The Flint begins as groundwater seepage in Hapeville, an Atlanta suburb about a hundred fifty miles north of Albany. A boater leaving there could travel three hundred fifty miles to the southwest corner of the state where the Flint, with the Chattahoochee River, forms Lake Seminole. It is uncommon among American rivers in that it flows unimpeded for more than two hundred miles. Along the route, both the land's beauty and history open up for all those willing to see.

Before white settlers pushed into Southwest Georgia in the early 1800s and founded Albany along the Flint, the Muskogee, or Creek, Indians called it Thronateeska, "flint picking-up place." Once the Indians were driven from the land they were born on, those same white settlers used the Flint to transport their cotton to market at the Gulf of Mexico. Water of life and water of commerce.

About a hundred years later the Flint was dammed near Cordele to generate electrical power, and the more than eight-thousand-acre Lake Blackshear was created. The lake and the river near it included hundreds of property owners who fished, boated, and partied along the waterways. It was the playground of the region. That's where I was headed after my telephone conversation with Tony Patrick. According to my source, it was becoming a dirty and killing playground.

Driving south on Jefferson Street in Albany, I turned onto Philema Road and a few miles outside of Albany crossed a bridge on Highway 32 with the Flint running underneath. I slowed my car and looked down at the greenish, low-running water and the cypress and water oaks lining the banks for miles.

There had been little rain during the summer and several big rocks and fallen trees and tree limbs usually covered by water were visible. The river was seasonably low. With no traffic behind me, I had slowed to fifteen miles an hour and looked on both sides of the river as if somebody had left something for me to see. I was looking at the river in a way I had never looked at it before. As if there were a revelatory mystery riding the slow waters below.

"I don't see anything dead. Looks about right to me. No dead alligators. No dead fish." I said in the same way I would've had somebody been riding with me.

I turned off the eight-track tape player and turned on the car radio and heard a CBS reporter quoting President Reagan's economic outlook for the remainder of 1983. I listened for a couple of minutes then turned that off, pushed the Dylan tape back in, and heard more music and thought about the times in college when I boated with friends on Lake Blackshear, twenty minutes up ahead. It's a beautiful lake and just a few minutes from where I attended college in Americus. Some of my college classmates had grown up on the lake and had taken me on boat rides and fishing trips there. I wasn't surprised by the flood of good memories driving to the lake that day.

Being hired by Mickey Burke the same day I walked into the newsroom with a few of the college newspaper stories I had written, now that did surprise me. Mickey knew who I was from his brother Ricky. Ricky and I played basketball together at the Albany YMCA. Only thing Mickey knew about me was that I was a pretty good athlete. He talked more about playing ball than he did newspapers my first day in the newsroom. The job interview lasted about five minutes, and he didn't ask to read my stories.

"Can you start next week?" Mickey said.

"Yes, sir. I can."

"Don't call me 'sir.' I'm Mickey. You got it?"

"Yes, sir…I mean, yes, Mickey."

"I'll see you Monday morning. Don't be late."

"Thanks, Mickey. I'll see you Monday."

My first full-time job interview lasted about as long as it took to insert a piece of paper into a typewriter. I was hired.

After crossing that bridge on the way to the river that day, I saw a man and a boy fishing in a flat-bottom aluminum boat in the backwaters near several tall cypress trees. The water was still all around them. The man looked to be about forty, and the boy maybe eight or nine. Anyone fishing mid-day in this heat must love being on the water, I thought. Then I thought about my dad and godfather taking me fishing when I was a boy in Indiana. Maybe one day I'd have a boy or two to do the same for. My godfather caught bass, bluegill, and trout and he, more so than my dad, believed fishing was part of God's plan for a man's eternal salvation. I looked away from the river and re-focused on the highway and my driving.

After a mile or so I turned north on Highway 300 that would take me to Tony Patrick's house, and the Flint River.

During another assignment last year on the Chattahoochee River, I was riding in a U. S. Coast Guard boat with my photographer and saw twelve-foot long alligators, metallic and ancient, sunning themselves along the water's edge. We were doing a story about the Coast Guard assignment along the Chattahoochee. Maybe today I'd see an alligator or two. They would have to be hard to kill.

The music played and the warm wind blew into my car and my mind rambled on, but didn't stay long in one place or on one story. I crossed Smoak Bridge and saw Lake Blackshear on both sides with the still water reflecting the sky, blue with a few clouds, and the sun overhead slanting its rays across the lake in a blinding way. I saw no boats on the water.

Ten minutes beyond the lake I turned onto a paved county road and into an area called Valhalla, a subdivision with two-story red-brick homes on one-acre lots. Most of the homes had boats in their driveways or yards. Some had two, one to fish in and one to drive pulling water-skiers. I looked at the paper that had Tony Patrick's address on it and found his house and pulled into the gravel driveway. It was an easy find.

I parked near a green aluminum flat-bottom boat that looked like the one I had seen earlier on the Flint with a man and a boy fishing from it. Plenty of room for two fishermen, I thought. There was a twenty-five horsepower motor on the boat. On both sides of the boat in three-inch black lettering was the name *Cheap Sunglasses*. A big man came out of the side door from the kitchen that led to the garage when I was getting out of my car. The two of us walked toward one another.

"Mr. Patrick, I'm John Maynard with the *Albany Chronicle*."

"Hell, call me Tony. The only people who call me Mr. Patrick are bill collectors and cops, and the DNR boys." When he was younger, Tony had gotten to know several of Georgia's Department of Natural Resources law enforcement officers for doing things on the river and lake that he shouldn't have. The mischief Tony had been involved in usually involved fast boats and lots of beer.

We shook hands.

"Okay, Tony."

Tony was thirty-five, a little over six feet, and his arms looked as if he had been used to lifting something heavy or splitting wood year-round. He had sandy brown hair, a darker mustache, and looked like a Jimmy Buffet stand-in. He could sing after a few beers, but not very well. When he did sing it wasn't Buffet and songs from the islands. It was ZZ Top, the Texas rock band whose members wore long beards, hats, and sunglasses. *Cheap Sunglasses* was the name of one of their songs.

In the garage there was a set of free weights and a line of rod and reels on both walls. There may have been a dozen on each side. Tony had enough to open his own sporting goods store, I thought.

"Are you ready?" Tony said.

"If you are, I am."

"All I need to do is hook up my boat, and we'll get out of here. I want you to see why I was runnin' hot on the phone. Hell, I've been runnin' hot for some time now. I want everybody to see."

Tony got into his white Ford pickup truck and backed up to *Cheap Sunglasses*. Inside the boat were two orange seat cushions, two brown wooden paddles, and a large red and white ice chest. He eased his truck two inches from the hitch on the boat and stopped. He got out of his truck and hitched the boat and attached the cords for the brake lights on the back of the trailer hitch. I offered to help.

"No, buddyro, I got it myself. Just give me a second. That's all I need. I been doin' this since I was five. Thanks, though. I got it."

Tony needed only a few seconds to get everything ready and when the trailer and boat were secured, I got in the cab of the truck with the two notepads and two pens. Tony got in the truck and reached behind his seat and picked up a straw hat with a red-tailed hawk feather in it and put the hat on his head. Then he pulled out of the driveway and we headed toward the Flint River.

After ten minutes of driving on paved county roads and a couple of dirt ones, Tony pulled into Camper's Haven along the river. There were small pop-up trailers and doublewides scattered along the bank under oak, cypress, and pine trees. A canopy of shade stretched throughout Camper's Haven. There was a general store, Gator Pit, with a boat launch. The store sold gas, crickets and minnows, hooks and bobbers, Vienna sausage, crackers, sardines, cold beer, beef jerky, honey buns, pork rinds, and other things a family might want on a daylong river trip. The Pit had it all for fun on the water.

A large sign over the store had a colored illustration of a giant alligator pulling the bikini bottoms off a beautiful young woman. Her bottoms were made like a Confederate flag. She was smiling and so was the gator.

Tony stopped next to the boat ramp, and I saw no other boat trailers in the parking area that could've accommodated a couple of dozen.

"Hop out, Mr. Reporter," Tony said. "Let me ease *Cheap Sunglasses* into the water and then we'll take off. Just give me a couple more minutes, and we'll be ready."

I got out of the truck and stood by a picnic table next to two large empty green trash barrels. Along the water there was a wooden stand and a hose where fisherman could clean their catch. The sun was baking the old wooden fish stand dry and gray, brittle almost. The picnic table and wooden stand were near two massive water oaks. The air was hot, as if it had been released from a giant campfire. Tony backed *Cheap Sunglasses* into the water, put his truck in park, got out, unhitched the boat from the trailer, and took a rope from the boat and tossed it to me. Then Tony stepped on top of the trailer and pushed the boat off it and into the water. He was gentle, as if there were a young child he was trying to protect.

Tony got back in his truck and slowly pulled away and parked the truck and trailer in the Gator Pit's empty parking lot. I used the rope to pull *Cheap Sunglasses* along the wooden dock that was old and needed replacing. I kept the boat steady as Tony got in.

"Okay, my man, ease on in here and throw me the rope," Tony said.

I followed his instructions. There were three bench seats in the boat, and Tony sat in the back to operate the motor and guide the boat and I sat up front. The ice chest stayed in the middle. Tony pulled the engine cord twice, and it started smoothly on the second pull, as if it had been warming up while Tony was driving the truck. A few miles south of the Gator Pit was Transpower Inc., and ten miles beyond that was Lake Blackshear. I had been on this part of the river several times before that day, but never looking for dead fish and dead alligators.

Tony cruised through the no-wake zone, causing the brownish backwater in the slough to turn over in a harmless way. We passed cypress trees, sometimes six to eight clustered together rising out of the water and holding nests for hawks and ospreys and other water birds. Along the river bank on a tree limb extending over the water, I saw six turtles in the sun and as *Cheap Sunglasses* passed by, the turtles fell one after another in the water, as if it were a choreographed routine they practiced daily. There were a few small white cotton clouds that provided no relief from the sun. Three minutes later we were out of the slough, beyond the no-wake zone and leaving Camper's Haven and the Gator Pit behind. The wind felt good to my face as Tony increased speed. A wide view of water and trees was now visible. Things had opened up.

Tony was on the big river now. He knew its moods, its bends, where the fish were and where they weren't from month to month. He had been reared along the river by parents who had taught him these things when he was a little boy. His father had taught him how to bait both a hook and a trotline and how to skin and deep-fry snapping turtles, and do the same with alligator tail. As a boy, he swam near the sandbars and wasn't bothered at all by the alligators in the sun fifty yards away. Early on he thought them more beautiful than dangerous. He believed that as man, too. By the time he was thirteen, he knew as much about the river as some men who had spent a lifetime fishing it. A day never passed without him touching the water when he was young, he said. He had a three-inch scar on his right forearm from twelve stitches where a forty-pound snapping turtle bit him one night while he was checking a trotline that had been baited with chicken gizzards. Tony was seventeen then, and Budweiser and marijuana had been allies of the gator turtle. The turtle fell into the water to freedom. Tony's blood followed the turtle.

He had some other markings from the river. He cut his feet on broken glass one night while camping along a sandy beach two miles south of Camper's Haven. He and his girlfriend were skinny-dipping at one in the morning. She drove him to the emergency room in Cordele after they put their clothes back on. A twenty-two pound catfish stung him one fall afternoon after Tony played him for thirty minutes on a reel with a ten-pound test line. That scar was still visible, too. When he was in his mid-twenties he was going much too fast in a small johnboat when the river was low. He hit a rock he didn't see and was tossed out of the boat and cut his forehead on another rock. It was nine stitches that time. He said it had only been two beers and no joints had he smoked. No one believed him about the beer and the joints. People along the river knew Tony. He said the river scarred his body in a sacred way. The same way Indian cultures used physical pain on boys as a rite of passage into manhood. Whatever amount of blood Tony had lost on the Flint River since he was a boy had shaped what kind of man he had become. This was easy for me to figure out.

Tony was not at full speed, allowing me to ask questions and write what he said and what I saw.

"How long have you been living near the river?"

"Since the day my momma brought me home from Sumter Regional Hospital in Americus. I'll never live anywhere else. Once you get this thing inside of you, it won't get out of you."

"Are you on it a lot?"

"Not every day, but about every week. And sometimes two or three times a week. Depends on the fishing. Depends on other things too. Stayed on it all the time when I was growing up. Always felt if I left it, something bad would happen to me. Always gave me a sick feeling if I went a couple of days without being on the water. Still does."

"What do you do for a living, Tony?"

"I sell real estate and have been for the last five years. Before that I worked construction and some of those houses in my neighborhood I helped build. And I make a little money fishin'. That's my love. I do a few bass tournaments each year."

"How's that?"

"Bass tournaments here and there. Back in the spring I won five thousand dollars at Lake Eufaula over in Alabama. There were two hundred and fifty other fishermen who wanted that money. It's a nice supplement to my income and a helluva a lot of fun. And John, it's *hard* to sell property up here now with this river the way it is."

"What about family?"

"Me and Rebecca got two boys. Jake's eight and Adam's five. My parents still live here. They're on Lake Blackshear now. I got a sister in Atlanta and a brother in Jacksonville. Good family. We all grew up on the water. I got from my dad same as he got from his."

"They don't have river-blood in them? Your brother and sister?"

"Just some I reckon. Not like me. Not near as much as me."

"Do you take your boys fishing? Do they like being on the river?"

"Well, hell, Mr. Reporter, what do you think? I thought you were smart and then you ask a question like *that*."

Tony looked at me, throttled down a little harder and smiled, cutting through the water faster now, heading south to Transpower Inc. The river was widening now, about two hundred feet across. The afternoon remained hot and still. No breeze blowing unless the boat was going. Near several palm plants there were three still and patient egrets waiting for fish to swim by for an afternoon meal. Along a patch of green reeds there were water birds, blue, white, and red, sitting and looking content with whatever might happen. I didn't know what kind they were other then majestic. I was looking for gators, but didn't see any, and kept taking notes of everything I saw.

"Another couple of minutes and we'll be there. That's when you'll see that shit I've been talkin' about," Tony said. He spoke loud enough for me to hear him clearly over the engine.

An osprey flew a hundred feet directly over the boat, and I turned around in my seat to watch the bird swoop down and lift a fish out of the water with its powerful claws. It looked like a catfish, but I wasn't certain. With the fish clutched, the osprey flew atop a cypress tree into a nest and began to stab into the fish with its beak, feeding the fish to two hatchlings. The boat moved further south.

I lost sight of the osprey, but my nose found something awful.

"What's that stench?"

Tony began to slow *Cheap Sunglasses*. There was a bend in the river up ahead.

"That's the smell of economic development. That's the smell of jobs. Hell, that's the smell of dead fish, dead turtles, dead ducks. It's killin' everything. God it makes me sick. You ain't seen shit yet. You're just smellin' it. Wait till you see it. You won't believe it when you see it."

Tony eased *Cheap Sunglasses* around the bend and the river straightened for the next two hundred yards. That's when I saw the two large discharge pipes pushing enormous amounts of waste into the river. The closer we got to the discharge pipes and the paper mill built by Transpower Inc., I began to see what I had smelled moments earlier.

The paper mill sat on the right bank, where the river was about a hundred fifty feet across, and north of Lake Blackshear. Tony stopped in the middle of the river at the discharge pipes. Half of the river, the half closest to the paper mill, had become black at the surface. An ugly black. The other half, extending to the opposite bank, was the natural color along that stretch of the Flint River. The color contrast was striking. The smell was sickening. I looked down river for several hundred yards and black covered half the river as it did adjacent to the plant. I could not see the end of the mess as the river began to bend, but I did see something else.

Along each bank south of the discharge pipes were floating dead fish. There were hundreds of largemouth bass, blue gill, red-belly sunfish, and catfish. All of them pooled together, rotting, with flies hovering over them. The more dead fish I saw, the worse the smell was.

"How far is it like this?"

"For the next mile or two and then after that you don't see as many. It smells like fifty thousand people shit in the river at the same time. Don't you think?"

"That's about right. How far are we from Lake Blackshear?"

"Around ten miles. Maybe a little more. Maybe a little less."

"What about the lake? What kind of condition is it in?"

"Well, you can't smell it there, and the water doesn't look any different than it did before the company began production. Those assholes. But it's going to change, too, if this keeps up. Unless we stop up those pipes, the lake is going to get it too."

I put my left hand over my nose and mouth and with my right clutched the red seat cushion on top of the aluminum bench as Tony sped up to get beyond the worst of it. I wished *Cheap Sunglasses* could go faster to get us the hell out of this awfulness.

"*Look over there!*" Tony said.

He pointed with his left hand to a thirty-yard stretch of light brown sand on the east bank, not far from the discharge pipes.

An adult raccoon was standing over what looked to be a smaller raccoon lying motionless in the sand. Five small raccoons were moving around the one that didn't move. The big raccoon nudged the one lying down as if to try to make it stand up. The big one nudged again with her nose. It was no use. Tony slowed the boat so we could get a better look.

"Raccoons eat clams and they're dying along this area because of whatever that black shit is coming out of those pipes," Tony said. "Now even the animals in the woods are dying. Damn those bastards!"

"You think so, Tony? Are you certain that what the company is putting in the river is killing these animals?"

"Hell, I don't know what to think anymore, but look at this. Smell this. How'd you like to live in it and eat your meals from it? That shit would kill you. What else is causing all this dyin' up? Is the whole thing going to die?"

Tony turned the hand throttle again, picking up speed, and soon we were about three miles from the pipes, and there were fewer dead fish. Still we saw some. The smell remained putrid. Tony cut a circle in the river and stopped altogether.

"Have you seen enough?"

"What else is there?"

"You've seen the worst of it."

"You ready to get out of here?"

"Yep, I'm tired of seeing this, but here's the deal, Mr. Reporter. We've got to go right back through that shit to get to the Gator Pit. You make sure you remember what you see here. Take all this back with you. Don't forget a *damn thing!* Are you ready?"

As Tony talked, I was writing down everything that I had seen including the details of the smell, the color of the water, and the many dead and dying animals. That part of the river was full of dying and death in an unnatural way. Was Transpower to blame?

"Let's get out of here. I'll hold my nose and get through it again. I've seen enough for now."

With that Tony used full speed to head back from where we had come, back to the Gator Pit. I thought about trying to count the dead fish, but that was an unreasonable idea. I would tell Mickey I had seen hundreds and hundreds. I had never seen anything like it before that day. Tony had gone a quarter of a mile when he saw something we had missed when we came down the river. He slowed and approached tangled tree limbs in the water on the west bank. There were four dead mallard ducks pressed up against the limbs. They were decaying with maggots running through their heads. They were once beautiful.

We passed the sandbar where we had seen the family of raccoons and now there was only one, lying in the sand, not moving at all. Its family had conceded death. Fifteen minutes later Tony turned his boat into the slough that led to Camper's Haven and the Gator Pit. He let off the throttle. I wrote again in my notepad, stopped after several sentences, and put the pad and pen in my front pants pocket.

"I want you to meet Lard Ass," Tony said.

"Who?"

"Lard Ass. He owns the Gator Pit. You need to meet him."

"That's his name? His real name?"

"Yeah, that's his name. What's wrong with that? You jealous you don't have a great name like that? His dad's name was Wide Lard Ass. It all makes sense, Mr. Reporter. You're probably jealous, aren't you?"

"Well, no, not really. I'm fairly satisfied with the name I have. I've grown to like it."

"His momma and daddy sure did bless him with a pretty name. Lard, I mean. Don't you think? It just has a beautiful sound to it. Don't you agree, Mr. Reporter?"

"I don't believe that's his *real* name, Tony. If I am going to quote him in a story about the river, I think my editor will want something besides *Lard Ass said yesterday the Flint River...*"

"How about r*eal* Lard Ass? Maybe you should quote him that way."

I gave up for the moment. Tony continued to guide *Cheap Sunglasses* toward the boat ramp. The parking lot was still empty, other than Tony's trailer and truck. A slow business day.

"His real name is Bubba Jackson, but we call him Lard and sometimes Lard Ass. Hell, he calls himself Lard. Done so since the sixth grade. A few years ago some boys with the Department of Natural Resources were removing a six-foot long gator from under an oak tree at Camper's Haven. They were having a helluva of time doin' so. Lard had just bought the store a few weeks earlier and called the DNR about the gator who seemed to like Camper's Haven more than the river. Those two DNR boys, scrawny little shits both of them, were gettin' whipped pretty good. They had a noose around the gator and wanted to tape his legs, but couldn't calm him. So Lard sat on top of the gator, and the boys wrapped him up. Just like a nice Christmas gift your momma would give you. The kind your momma used to wrap. Then Lard picked him up, the gator that is, all by himself and threw that sucker in the back of their DNR truck."

"This Lard Ass must be a pretty strong guy."

"Yep, then one of those DNR boys looked at him and said, 'Sometimes it's good to have a lard ass.' Before that, he was just Lard. That was it, Mr. Reporter, my friend. That's where it all came from. After that, instead of Lard, he was *Lard Ass*. Don't you like that better? Isn't that a better name?"

"He sounds like a guy I need to meet."

Tony stopped the boat, giving me a place to step out of it onto the gray wooden dock. I carried the rope with me that was tied to *Cheap Sunglasses*. Then Tony got out of the boat and walked through the parking lot and got into his truck and backed the trailer down the ramp. He got out of the truck, backed into the boat and drove it onto the trailer. After Tony secured the boat on the trailer and pulled away from the ramp and parked, we went inside the Gator Pit to see Bubba Jackson. I mean Lard Ass.

The Gator Pit was a cinder block building from the early 1950s, and it had a window air conditioning unit and a plywood floor. There were mounted largemouth bass on the walls and one deer head, a wild hog head, a stuffed bobcat, and a *Playboy* calendar from 1975, the year I got out of high school. A few years after Lard Ass did. I didn't recognize the Bunny on the calendar, but looked at it for a few seconds trying to.

Lard was behind the counter near the cash register, and he was wearing a gray cap that said 'Possums Do It Upside Down.' On his cap was an illustration of two possums screwing, and both had smiles of equal contentment. He had a white T-shirt on, jeans, and was smoking a Chesterfield. Lard was five feet nine, maybe, but every bit of two hundred seventy-five pounds. I could see he would be plenty helpful to anyone trying to subdue an angry alligator. I could see now why Bubba was Lard.

"Lard, I want you to meet John Maynard. He's a reporter from the *Albany Chronicle*. He came to see our fucked up river. Be nice to him. Maybe he'll try to help us."

"Well, I'll be a damn sumbitch. I never before met a real live reporter. Does he bite, Tony? Has he had all of his shots? Does he have two balls like the rest of us? Never seen a real one before. Feed a monkey and watch him shit."

"He hasn't bitten me yet, and I haven't asked him how many balls he has."

I shook hands with Lard Ass.

"Good to meet you Lard. How you doing today?"

"Well, not worth a shit since they put the pipes in and screwed our river up. I'd like to stick one of those pipes up their ass. And since they put those pipes in our river – well, do you see any boat trailers out there?"

He pointed to his parking lot with only the middle finger of his right hand.

I took my notepad and pen from my pocket and put the pad on the counter in front of Lard.

"How long has it been like this? Your business, I mean."

"I suppose about four weeks now. Some folks still come up and go north to fish. Money-wise I'm off probably seventy-five percent of what I usually take in this time of year. I do know that. Feed a monkey and watch him shit."

I asked Lard a few questions about his life growing up in nearby Americus and spending a lot of time as a boy and a man fishing and boating on the river. I got good quotes I could use in my story.

"Have you called anyone with the state's Environmental Protection Division or the EPA? Have you guys contacted anybody with the state or feds?"

"We've called them," Lard said. "Well, no, Tony called them. Not me. I ain't talked yet to no sumbitch but you."

"Yeah, they sent a couple of men down here, and I met with them," Tony said. "They took some notes and took a boat ride and said they'd get back to us."

"Who?" I said. "Who came down from where?"

"Two guys from the EPD in Atlanta," Tony said. "I'm waiting to hear what their next move is going to be. If they have a next move."

"That's right," Lard said. "And we're getting tired of waiting. The longer we wait, the more money I lose. Hell, the longer we wait, the more the river dies. Damn shame. Feed the monkey and watch him shit."

"Did you contact anybody with the federal government?" I said.

"No," Tony said. "I'm waiting to see what the state is going to do. The EPA may be next."

"Tony, can you give me the names of who you've spoken with at the EPD?"

"I got them written down. I'll give them to you later."

"I'll tell you one thing Jake," Lard said. "Is it Jake or Jack? I forgot. What the hell is it?"

"It's John. John Maynard."

"Okay, John, you can write this down and put it in your newspaper. Anybody who screws up our river ought to have their nuts eaten off by a snapping turtle, one slow bite at a time. I mean those boys from Transpower. Yep, that's who I'm talkin' about. I'd be happy to hold them down and let the turtle snap away. Put that in your damn paper!"

"Okay, Lard. We'll print that in big, bold print. Above the fold, I'm sure."

"Lard, we got to take off," Tony said. "John here's got to get back and put what you said on the front page. I just wanted you to meet him. We'll find out how many balls he has later."

"Well, I hope I am on the front page. I damn sure should be. Come back and see me sometime."

"I will. Good to meet you, Lard. Hey, Lard, I got one more question. What does 'feed a monkey watch him shit' mean?"

"That's what my daddy would say when he was playin' poker."

We shook hands again and Tony and I walked out of the Gator Pit to his truck and boat. Tony reached inside the boat and pulled two cold beers out of the ice chest, and we sat at a picnic table under the shade of an oak tree and drank them. We talked more about his life, family, and the Flint. I took more notes, filling more than half of one of my notebooks. We got into Tony's truck and drove to his house.

After Tony pulled into his driveway, he gave me the names of the state environmentalists he had spoken with, and I wrote them down. I got out of the truck and Tony picked up his Styrofoam ice chest and headed toward his garage, and a storage room connected to it.

"Come back here a few minutes before you go."

"Okay."

I followed Tony to the storage room where there were several rods and reels hanging on the walls, pictures of big largemouth bass that Tony had caught, a twelve-pounder mounted, a ZZ Top concert poster from Atlanta in 1974, and an eight-track tape player and two black wooden speakers. Two lawn chairs were set up in the room.

Tony opened the ice chest and took out two more beers.

"This is the inner sanctum," Tony said.

He handed me another beer and ice fell off the can onto the floor.

"Just one more then I got to get on the road. But they sure taste good, Tony. Don't want to over-do it. I do like my job."

"I understand. One more won't hurt you."

"Yep, heard that before."

We popped the beers together and took a big gulp and then another. I looked at the walls in the inner sanctum and at the many pictures of Tony, his friends, his pretty wife, and two sons. There were pictures of him and his boys fishing and camping along the part of the river that was now covered with death. In a couple of the pictures they were playing in the water, big smiles everywhere.

"I think Lard's right," Tony said.

"Right about what?"

"Anybody that does *that* to our river, any river, ought to have their nuts eaten off by a mean-ass turtle. Don't you agree?"

"That would get their attention all right. I agree with that."

"Damn sure would. I'm like Lard. I'd help hold the bastards down."

"I'd like to see it."

"I'd like to do it."

We both took another drink of beer.

"Tony, what's next for you? What's going to happen up here?"

"I'll do what it takes to get our river back where it should be. First, I want to know why nothing is being done now to stop what's happening. And then I'm going figure out what I have to do to stop it. People up here are ready to organize and fight to stop what that company's doing to us. Hell, we're mad. Have every right to be mad."

I wrote down more quotes and took another drink from the cold beer.

"Have you talked to anyone with Transpower about what they are doing to the Flint? What do they say?"

"Yeah, I've talked to some PR prick a couple of times. I'll give you his name and number. He was about useless. What do you expect them to say? *We're not really killing your river, it's just your imagination.* Or how about this. *It's not that bad. We just need some rain.*"

Tony took a pen and piece of paper from a cabinet drawer in the inner sanctum and wrote down the information and gave it to me. I took the paper, looked at it, and folded it and placed it in my pocket.

"Thanks. And thanks for the beer. I've got to get home, but I'll be in touch."

"I hope so. Maybe what you're doing will help. I hope it does."

"I'll meet with my editor in the morning, and I'll call you to let you know how we're going to handle the story. There's a hell of a lot here, Tony. This is a mess. Your river's a mess."

"It's our river, Mr. Reporter. Not just mine. It's our river."

"You're right. Yeah, you're right about that."

"Call anytime. I usually leave the house around eight or eight thirty. I work out of a Cordele office. Here's my number."

Tony handed me his business card with both his home and work numbers on it.

"Take care, Tony."

"You too, Mr. Reporter."

We shook hands, and I got in my car and headed back to Albany. It was close to six o'clock and still above ninety-five degrees. Not once on that boat ride had I thought about the heat.

# CHAPTER 3

Driving south back to Albany, I thought about the last few months at the *Chronicle* and how they'd been better than the first few after I was hired. In the beginning it was all re-writing press releases from the chamber of commerce, businesses, and politicians, and taking obituaries over the telephone from funeral homes in Moultrie, Thomasville, Bainbridge, Fitzgerald, and other places in Southwest Georgia. Good training maybe, but not much fun. Nothing of any significance.

As the weeks passed and my writing and reporting improved, with Mickey's profanity-laced critiques diminishing, I had been given more freedom to find and write stories on my own. I was assigned news and feature stories, and occasionally Mickey placed my stories on the front page. It was a good feeling to see my name in print and something worthwhile after it.

Then I thought about Abby Sinclair. The *Chronicle* had hired her about four months earlier, after she graduated with a degree in journalism from Valdosta State College, a hundred miles south of Albany. She worked upstairs in the features section, but wanted to be a news reporter. Mickey had no opening for her downstairs, he said. I had been thinking about her a lot lately, and began doing so the first time I saw her walk into the newsroom to get a roll of film from a photographer. She was striking. Dark eyes and dark hair, and a smile that once I saw it, well, that was all I had been seeing. Even when I wasn't around her.

We talked news occasionally at work, and a week ago had drinks together at Yesterday's, a good local restaurant that most nights turned into a good bar. Before the drinks came, I had gotten lost in her and the way she tilted her head, and in the way she talked about books and music. She knew all the words to Bob Dylan's "Tangled Up in Blue." She read poets I had never heard of and talked about them as if she had grown up with them. She followed the news of the day and had a sharp curiosity about the world that made her even more attractive to me. I told myself driving home from the river that day I would try to talk to her in the morning, and tell her about the story I was on. I knew she would appreciate the telling of it.

During my ride back to Albany, I crossed the bridge where, earlier, I had seen a man and a boy fishing together in a flat bottom boat on the Flint. I saw them again. They had pulled their boat out of the water on a ramp near the highway. The man was securing the fishing poles and ice chests. The shirtless, sun-tanned boy was grinning as he carried a stringer of catfish, maybe twelve or fifteen, to the man, who put them in an ice chest. The best I could see after slowing to about ten miles an hour, they were a pound or two each. It had been a good day on the river for them.

I ought to call her tonight, I thought, not wait till the morning to tell her. I had her telephone number. Maybe I should call her later and tell her about what I saw and heard on my river trip. That would give her something to think about and something for us to talk about. With Abby, though, there was always something to talk about. She would appreciate the story I was on. And I would appreciate seeing her.

She was from Albany, but lacked the smugness that infected some of the girls she covered at the debutante balls, whose outlook centered on themselves and the huge amounts of money they believed they needed to make themselves happy. Their false happiness could easily turn to misery. Abby Sinclair was not that way. Her father James was a construction man. He built things with his hands. He worked hard and didn't have the money to spoil Abby and her brother David, and even if he did, he wouldn't have done it, she said.

Her mother Rachel had been reared in a cotton-mill family from Opelika, Alabama. For Rachel, the sun never set without her memory recalling the poverty of her youth with a clarity that she could still see and taste and feel. They were always poor growing up. Her refrain to Abby, "Remember what little you have has nothing to do with how much love you can give." Abby's mother didn't work outside the home, but took care of it, her children, and her husband. And she read books. Caldwell, Welty, and Faulkner were her favorites, and those books spoke to her, offering strength and sustenance and an understanding of her own childhood. And the land her people had walked upon. She passed the reading on to Abby, who went through them in the same sustaining manner. One book followed another. Poets had the same effect on her. I needed to call her.

When I got home my roommate had left me a note saying he was at Jim's Oyster Bar and asking me to join him for a beer. I thought about going, but didn't. I took a cold shower and pulled a cold beer from the refrigerator and turned the television on to the evening news. I had not seen anything on television or in another newspaper about what was happening on the Flint. It seemed I would break the story. Mickey was going to be excited when I told him about it in the morning, I thought.

I finished the beer and turned off the television and picked up the book I had been reading about revolutions in Central America, and how the U.S. government had for decades been supporting vicious dictators as long as they proclaimed anti-communism. It was a sickening story, like the dead fish on the river. I read it for thirty minutes and then picked up the telephone.

"Hello."

"Abby, this is John Maynard."

"Hey, how are you? I didn't see you this afternoon when I came down to the newsroom. Where were you?"

"Mickey sent me on an assignment after lunch."

"Where'd you go?"

"I went up to the Flint River south of Cordele. It was about fifteen miles north of Lake Blackshear. I took a boat ride with a guy named Tony Patrick. You'd like him. It was some trip. I promise you that."

"That's a nice assignment. A boat ride. Why can't I get an assignment like that? I know that part of the river and it's beautiful up there. My dad used to take us on boat rides up there when I was little. Very pretty place. Poetic, I think."

"There's more to it than that. There's a story there. There's definitely a story. But I did go on a boat ride."

"What's the story, John?"

"What are you doing tonight?"

"I'm not doing anything. I have no plans. What's the story? Tell me."

"I can't tell you."

"What do you mean you can't tell me? Why can't you tell me? Top secret. CIA maybe. You working for the federal government, John? Maybe even a double-agent?"

"No, not like that. I can tell you, of course I can. But I want to do it over drinks. How about Yesterday's?"

"Okay. I'd love to."

"Can you be ready in an hour?"

"Sure."

"I'll pick you up then. Okay?"

"Okay, John. I'll see you in a little while."

I hung up the telephone, stretched out on the beige sofa, closed my eyes and tried to sleep for a few minutes. I could not. I wanted to call Mickey and tell him about what I had seen on the river, but I didn't. That would have to wait. I turned the television back on to MTV and saw Michael Jackson singing. Wasn't interested in that, and turned it off.

I picked up the notepad that I had on the river and began flipping through the pages too fast to read them. I then went to my bedroom where I kept a manual black Royal typewriter, like the one I used in the newsroom. It was sitting on a white desk my father had painted for me the week after I was hired at the newspaper. I put a piece of tan paper in the typewriter and began typing what Tony Patrick and Lard Ass had said and what I had seen and smelled on the Flint that afternoon. I wanted to see the quotes in full.

My sentences made short concise paragraphs and they included the dead and dying fish, and the raccoon that was alone and dead on the beach. I spent a few minutes typing and developing my notes and adding questions I needed to ask the contacts Tony had given me. Tomorrow morning at the office I would use the names and telephone numbers I had gotten. Wonder where and when Mickey would run the story, I thought.

I left my typed papers and notepad on my desk, changed clothes, made a ham and cheese sandwich, ate in five minutes with a glass of iced tea, and left the house to pick up Abby. It was almost nine when I drove down Dawson Road to Shoreham Apartments where Abby lived alone. I stopped my car next to her blue Plymouth Duster, got out and walked up to her door and rang the doorbell. In a few seconds she opened the door.

She had on tan shorts and a white sleeveless blouse, and her dark eyes and dark hair were the way I remembered them from the first time I had seen her in the newsroom. My thoughts about her had not gone away since that day.

"You look great, and it's good to see you tonight," I said.

"Thanks. I've been thinking about you. And not just because of what you told me earlier on the phone."

"Too much thinking can get you in trouble. Don't you know that's what *they* say? You didn't learn that in school, Abby?"

"No, didn't learn that. But I've heard it said many times. Didn't take with me, though."

"I bet you never listen to *they*, do you, Abby?"

"Never have and never will."

"They can be wrong a lot."

"I want to listen to you. I want you to tell me all about this big story from your boat ride. I want to know everything. Why couldn't you tell me over the phone? Are you going to tell me now? Are you really working for the CIA? You don't look like a secret agent."

"Yeah, I do work for the CIA. They pay more than the paper."

"Please tell me what you did today."

"Easy. Don't be a pushy reporter. People won't like you that way."

"That's what I want to be. And that's what I'm going to be. So start talking."

We walked to my car and got in.

"Let's go to Yesterday's and have a drink, and we'll talk there. How about that?" I said.

"Why don't you tell me on the way?"

"No, let's wait."

"You're no fun, John. I knew it when I met you. Please be fun tonight."

"Well, fun is not the purpose. You're a reporter. Be patient."

I could see her smile as I drove out of her parking lot down Dawson Road to Yesterday's. It was a five minute drive. We parked, got out, and walked into the restaurant.

I shook hands with Woody the doorman, and he said good evening to Abby in a dignified manner. Woody was wearing black slacks, a pressed white long-sleeve shirt, a jacket, and no tie. He had a black beard, neatly trimmed, and black hair parted on the right side. Everything was always in place.

"John, I see you got this beautiful woman with you again tonight. You are truly a lucky man, my friend. Living a charmed life."

"Yes, indeed, Woody. Very lucky. I can't help it if I'm lucky."

"Abby, you've made John a lucky man tonight," Woody said.

"Luck is overrated, Woody," Abby said. "Decent, intelligent, well-read, now all of that is better than being lucky."

"You may be right, but he's still lucky."

People were coming in, the place was filling up and most of the tables were occupied. Couples were standing and drinking and talking along the black, thick wooden bar with a song by Fleetwood Mac, "Dreams," playing throughout. I wanted a table and asked Woody to find one for us.

"Follow me," Woody said.

He took us upstairs and found a table for two. A waitress came and we ordered drinks. Red wine for Abby and a beer for me.

After the waitress left, Abby said, "Now talk. I've waited long enough. I don't care if it is a CIA secret. Tell me everything. I want to know everything. I don't care if you're a double agent. Give me the truth."

I began with the telephone call to Tony Patrick in the newsroom that morning and told her everything, including the name of his boat, *Cheap Sunglasses*. She followed my story in the same way I listened to my father and his friends talk about the Great Depression and World War II. Every word she held on to. I described the dead animals and the smell, and the sight of the river in such a way that Abby's stomach was tightening, she said. Then the waitress brought our drinks. She took a slow sip of wine, and I did the same with my beer.

"Start a tab?"

"Yeah, we'll probably drink at least another one," I said.

"Okay. I'll check on y'all in a bit."

"Thanks," I said.

Abby set her wine class on the table and leaned toward me.

"I want to go see everything you saw. You got to take me up there the next time you go. Will you take me, John? You will, won't you? What kind of people would allow that to happen to our river? I've just got to see this myself."

"Yes, to your first question, and to your second question, I don't know, but I'm going to find out."

"So Mickey doesn't know any of this yet?"

"No, I didn't get back in town until late. I didn't go by the office. He'll know by eight in the morning. He'll decide what to do then."

"And you don't think anyone has reported on this? Has it been on WALB?" Abby said, referring to the local television station. "Or in any other papers?"

"Tony said no. I haven't heard anything about it until today. And you haven't."

"Big story, Johnny Boy. I know you're excited. You got to be excited. It's your biggest story so far I bet. Isn't it?"

She was right about all of that. That was the first time she had called me Johnny Boy. I liked the way she said it.

"Johnny Boy?"

"You don't like that? I'm sorry . . ."

"No, no, Abby. I think I do. Only when you say it."

"Just between you and me, and nobody else."

"It's a deal."

We both took another drink and set our glasses on top of the brown wooden table. The place was almost full now. People drinking and talking everywhere. More music by Fleetwood Mac and then the

Eagles. Typical night at Yesterday's.

"Abby, I wish you could've been with me today. It was awful, but I wish you could've seen it."

"Me too. Me too, Johnny Boy."

We talked some more about what I saw and heard that afternoon and had two more drinks. I paid the waitress, and we left Yesterday's about eleven. I drove her back home. A three-quarter moon rose high over Lake Loretta, a small city-lake near her apartment. From there I could see the moon and the lake, a place where lovers hold hands and fathers take little boys fishing. I parked again outside her apartment and got out and walked her to the door. I thought about kissing her and hoped she was thinking the same.

"Abby, thanks for listening to me tonight. I enjoyed telling you about this story."

"I've never heard a CIA agent talk so much."

"Was it too much?"

"No, remember John, it's girls that talk too much. That's what all the guys say. Right? If I had your story I'd be talking a lot, too. I'm glad you called me. And if not that story, we would've found *something* to talk about, Johnny Boy. Don't you think?"

"Yeah, we would've I'm sure."

"I'll see you tomorrow, John."

"Good night, Abby. See you tomorrow."

I watched her unlock the door and go inside and close the door behind her. I looked at the moon over the lake before getting into my car and wondered if looked that way over the Flint River. And I wondered why in the hell I hadn't kissed her. She was thinking the same thing alone inside her apartment.

# Chapter 4

I arrived at the newsroom at seven thirty the next morning, wanting to talk to Mickey before other reporters and editors got there. Mickey was sometimes early, sometimes not. When I opened the heavy glass door to the *Chronicle,* I saw one other reporter and Mickey sitting at his desk drinking coffee, smoking a cigarette, and reading the *Atlanta Constitution.* He had on the same clothes he was wearing yesterday, hair that needed washing, and a face that needed shaving. Sometimes his after work drinks lasted until the next morning. He looked and smelled the part.

Mickey sometimes had martinis at Madeline's, a bar and restaurant a block from the newsroom, after he left the office in the afternoon. Then more drinks at other places. If he didn't make it home to his wife and children, well, he probably slept somewhere for a little while. Mickey could often be edgy after a night of drinking in full. A fast-talking-tell-me-quickly-what-you-know-no-bullshit editor. Too many martinis and little sleep would make any man edgy.

"Maynard, where the hell you been? And goddamnit, tell me about what you found out yesterday at the river. Let's hear it."

Mickey's bloodshot eyes penetrated my clear ones. Mickey's fire flamed quickly, but could ease just as fast. Stay calm with clarity of language.

"I met Tony Patrick and we . . ."

"Who in the hell's Tony Patrick?"

"Mickey, that's the contact you gave me. The guy you spoke with yesterday about the Flint River. You gave me his name and number. He's my source. He's the one who called the newsroom."

Mickey looked across the almost empty newsroom, took a daylong pull from his cigarette, and flipped ashes into the Vietnam ashtray. He'd probably smoked a hundred since yesterday.

"Maynard, I remember *exactly* what I told you. Now you tell me something I don't know."

I told him everything I learned from yesterday, but it was a quick version, probably less than two minutes. That's the way Mickey liked it. When it was over, Mickey asked a few questions that I had not yet considered about the story. He was always perceptive about newspaper stories and the people who read them and the people who wrote them. I would miss things, but not Mickey.

"I want you to call each of those contacts this Tony Patrick gave you. And get me some good quotes. Get a little background on if Transpower has dumped shit in other rivers. Do your research. Make it tight. I want some quotes from Fat Ass, or whatever his name is, about hurting his business. What's the damn boy's *real* name?"

"Bubba Jackson."

"I want this story on my desk by this afternoon. We'll run it tomorrow morning. You understand me?"

"I got it Mickey. It'll be ready."

That was what I wanted to hear and what I thought I'd hear. I left Mickey's desk and walked to my own with names, telephone numbers, and typed notes from last night. I dialed the first number on my list.

Eugene Harris was the public relations spokesman for Transpower Inc. at the Crisp County plant, where the river had turned black. He answered his telephone at nine ten. I had pen in hand and notepad opened to a clean, lined page. I identified myself and asked Harris to respond to the dead animals, black water, and angry river men like Tony Patrick and Bubba Jackson. I didn't say Lard Ass. I spoke clearly. A slow cadence with each word.

"Mr. Harris, what is it your company is dumping into the Flint River?"

"Treated discharge from our plant that employs five hundred people in our area. Good paying jobs. All of them. More money than most of these hard-working folks have ever made."

"Yes sir, I understand that. But what is it exactly that's killing fish and other animals south of your plant?

"Mr. Maynard, I don't know what you're talking about. I know the river is low right now and may look different. But our plant isn't killing anything. We have a permit from the Georgia Environmental Protection Division and are following all state and federal laws. We are in compliance, I assure you of this, with every law and regulation."

"Have you been on the river lately? Have you seen the fish kill and the discoloration? It smells awful and it's black as black coffee."

"No, Mr. Maynard, I haven't seen the river lately."

"So your position is the company has nothing to do with the fish kill and the fact that the river is black for miles past your discharge pipes? Several miles."

"That's right. The river is low. When the fall and winter rains come the water level will rise again. If there are dead fish and places where the water *looks* black well . . . we've nothing to do with that. Transpower didn't cause any of that. I can promise you that Mr. Maynard."

"Mr. Harris can you tell me specifically what's coming out of those pipes dumping into the river?"

"Like I said, it's treated discharge from the plant. We return water that we use to manufacture paper towels, disposable diapers, and other products that people need. And all of that produces good paying jobs."

"Yes, sir, I understand about the good paying jobs. But there has to be something in that water that's killing those fish."

In my mind, I saw the ducks with maggots running through their heads.

"Mr. Maynard, I have said all I know and I've answered all your questions. As I said, we are following all state guidelines. Would you like to know about our next employee picnic?"

"No sir. Thanks anyway."

I wanted to say other things about this man's indifference to how the river looked and smelled, and the dead animals floating on the surface. But I didn't. I got some quotes and that's all I needed for now.

"Mr. Maynard, I'll talk to you anytime. That's my job. I'll be happy to help you. I'm telling you everything I know."

"Thank you, Mr. Harris. I sure appreciate it. If I need more information, I'll get back to you."

"Anytime, Mr. Maynard. Glad to help any way I can."

Some help. I hung up the telephone. Mickey was standing over me, looking at me as if I had done something wrong. I knew the look.

"We need art. I want some art with this story, and I'm missing two photographers. They're both out of town on assignments. Both of them, damn it."

I thought of Abby and the fact that she was a better photographer than I was. I had seen enough of her work to know that. I remembered her fascination with the story last night at Yesterday's.

"Mickey, let's see if we can use Abby Sinclair from upstairs. She's a better photographer than me, anyway. I'll finish the story and call Tony Patrick, and he'll take us up the river. We'll be back with the art before you leave. She'll get some good art."

Mickey rubbed his black-stubbled chin three times. He lit another cigarette. The first pull was strong, as if there was some place he was trying to go and it was difficult getting there.

"Okay. I'll call the styles department and see if she's available this afternoon. You got a lot of shit to do. You better hustle, Maynard. Get the quotes right. I want all the sources you can get this morning."

Mickey returned to his desk, picked up the telephone, and called Lucille Webb, features editor. She agreed to allow Abby to go with me to the Flint. Mickey walked back to me. I was reading what I had written from the interview with Eugene Harris. He told me it was set with Abby and reminded me again I had a lot of work to do. The pressure felt good.

I called Tony, who agreed to meet us at the Gator Pit at one thirty. Good, I thought, time to write, then be with Abby.

Next, I called Stan Goodman with the state's Environmental Protection Division and got remarks similar to what the company man had said. There was no urgency in his voice for either how or why the river got to be the way it was south of the plant, or what was going to be done about it. But he gave me something new.

"Mr. Maynard, we've had several complaints from down there recently about water quality and in the next couple of weeks the EPD is going to begin taking water samples and testing. The public will be informed of our results, but it'll probably take about a month or so. Maybe longer."

"Is Transpower Inc. violating environmental laws?"

"No sir, Mr. Maynard, Transpower Inc. has a good environmental record all over the country. As of now they meet all the state and federal standards. They've been a good steward of natural resources."

"Have you seen the river during the past three weeks?"

"No, I was down there back during the spring with a team from our office. Everything looked good. They had just started production some weeks earlier. They were following all state regulations then, and I'm confident they are now."

"Well, not now. Everything does not look good now. That part of the river, south of the plant, looks and smells awful. Like death."

"Yes, sir. That's what we are hearing up here in Atlanta. There's just no reason for people to get too excited right now. We are going to look into the complaints. The EPD is going to do our job. I promise you that."

"Did you speak with Tony Patrick?"

"I did. More than once. He was a little excited. I'm sure everything is going to be okay, though," Goodman said. "I know the water level is low and that affects the oxygen for fish. But that will change when we get rain. Again, the company not only meets, but surpasses environmental standards."

I asked a few more questions before ending the interview with Stan Goodman. I got quotes to use, including the lead about the EPD's plans to test the water quality. Now the state was on record about their latest course of action, and the complaints they'd received from Tony Patrick and others living along the river and lake.

During the next few minutes I read the quotes from both telephone interviews and wondered what the two men would've said differently had they been looking at the same part of the river I had seen yesterday. Would that have made any difference in how they responded to my questions? What they said and how they said it did not temper the images from my boat ride with Tony.

Justin Blackwood answered my telephone call at the Environmental Protection Agency's regional office in Atlanta. Last week he had spoken with some property owners along Lake Blackshear and was making plans to visit the Flint River next week. "Transpower has been a good friend to the environment," he said, repeating a line I had already heard. Some friend. My interview with Blackwood lasted less than ten minutes, and I told him I would follow up after his visit to the river. I got more quotes to use in my story.

I hung up after my third telephone interview that morning and put a piece of typing paper in my typewriter. I had replaced the ribbon yesterday, giving the print a clean, crisp look. I began to type the story using my five sources and the things that I saw and smelled yesterday on the water with Tony. I included quotes from Lard Ass, of course, using his real name, Bubba Jackson, at the Gator Pit. The writing of it was not difficult.

I had had in my head the lede and the right sequence for the quotes and where to include the descriptions of the dead animals, and the putrid way the water smelled. All of it came out easily, as if it had been stored correctly and mechanically opened. There was no waiting involved. About two hours passed, and it seemed like fifteen minutes. I felt good about what I had done, and left my desk to buy a Coke out of the office machine. I was almost finished with what I had started writing. I walked around the newsroom, drank, and spoke to a few of the other reporters, some working on stories, others talking among themselves. The break felt good.

After thirty more minutes of writing and re-writing, I was satisfied and stopped. I was finished with the story. Mickey was away from his desk, but I walked over to it and put my story, seven pages taped together, nearly thirteen hundred words, in a wire basket on top of Mickey's desk. Mickey would probably cut some of the story, I thought. He'd make it better. He always did.

It was twelve forty-five when Abby walked from upstairs into the newsroom and over to my desk.

"Are you ready?" she said.

"Let's go."

She had a Nikon camera draped over her right shoulder and two rolls of black and white film, twenty-four exposures each, in her purse. I got up and we walked out of the newsroom together and got into my car. No air conditioning. It would be another hot drive. Not the way to impress Abby, I thought. But she wasn't impressed by those kinds of things anyway.

"Did you get your quotes this morning? Did you get everything you needed, John? Did you finish your story?"

"Yeah, I did. I did three interviews. The EPD, EPA, and some guy named Harris from the company, who wanted to talk about the next company picnic instead of why the fish are dying and why the river smells as bad as it does. I used Tony and a few things Lard Ass told me. I mean Bubba Jackson. The story's on Mickey's desk. It's kind of long. He'll cut some of it."

"You should've quoted *Lard Ass*. That would be a great headline. 'Lard Ass Says Business off from Fish Kill and Says He'll Sit on Company Officials Till They Stop Breathing.'"

"That's right, we want Lard Ass in thick bold print above the fold."

"Well, who wouldn't? That kind of headline wins awards. Don't you think, Johnny Boy?"

"Of course it does. Sell a million copies, too."

I turned on the radio and we heard an Elton John song from the album *Tumbleweed Connection*, "Where to Now St. Peter?" I heard every word clearly with Abby sitting next to me. *'I took myself a blue canoe/And I floated like a leaf/Dazzling, dancing half enchanted… Crazy was the feeling/restless were my eyes.'* Time passed and we talked about the story and other things as I drove to Camper's Haven and the Gator Pit. A few minutes later we saw Tony with *Cheap Sunglasses* already in the water. He had been waiting.

There were no other boat trailers in the parking lot. I parked near Tony's truck and Abby and I got out and walked to the boat ramp. I introduced Abby to Tony, and he helped her into the boat. We took off through the slough, going easy with no wake behind us. Tony again in charge.

"Abby, how long have you been in the news business?" Tony said.

"Just a few months. Not as long as John. I just got out of school at Valdosta."

"Well, you probably haven't seen anything like what you're about to see. I hope you've never seen anything like this. It's a mess up here."

"No, from what John told me last night, I haven't. I used to come up here with my family when I was a girl. We had a lot of fun on the water here."

Abby was wearing sunglasses, and the camera was hanging from her neck. I had taken my white shirt and tie off and was wearing a white T-shirt and a ball cap. Now I couldn't see Abby's eyes, but had not stopped thinking about them. It felt good, being with her again.

Tony cut through the slough with the sun high and entered the main body of the Flint pressing faster toward Transpower Inc., and the pipes in the river. After a few minutes we were there. Abby began taking pictures when the awfulness came into full view. She clicked the camera and said nothing. She kept clicking, eyes tight and firm on everything she was seeing and feeling.

"Tony can you pull over to that bank and stop? I want to get out," Abby said.

She pointed to the right side of the river fifty yards beyond the plant.

"Sure. Whatever you say, Miss Reporter."

Hundreds of dead fish were pressed against the bank, and the smell was as bad as it was yesterday. Tony headed for the spot she pointed to.

"Abby, it's a mess around here," I said. "You sure you want to get out of the boat?"

"I want a picture of Tony and those dead fish and those black rings of water bubbling up. I want that shot right here."

"Okay, but let's hurry," I said. "This smell will make us all sick. Soon we'll be dead like those fish."

Tony guided the boat through a mess of dead fish, largemouth bass and blue gill, some catfish, big ones too, and stopped along the sandy bank. I got out of the boat first, then helped Abby. Tony stayed in the boat while Abby took his picture. She shot a roll of film and hardly breathed the whole time because of the smell. Then we got back in the boat and Tony sped upriver back to the Gator Pit. Tony eased along the dock and Abby and I jumped out, said goodbye to Tony, and hurried to my car to get back to the newsroom so Mickey could decide what pictures he wanted for tomorrow's paper. We had left the *Chronicle* about ninety minutes earlier. I drove away from the Gator Pit with Abby by my side again. We would be back in the office in forty-five minutes. It was just like I planned.

"My dad used to take us for boat rides on that same spot on the river," Abby said. "I remember a couple of times we camped out on the *same* beach. It was my whole family. We had a lot of fun. One trip we found a handful of beautiful arrowheads. My dad still has them. What a mess now, John. It's just awful."

"If you go for a boat ride now you better wear a mask so you don't breathe that smell in and blinders so you don't see the dead fish. Some boat ride."

"Damn, it's so shameful what's happening, John. How could this be? How could people be this cruel? People just don't care about beauty. Is that it? What kind of people destroy beauty? *Bastards!*"

That was the first time I had heard her spice her language in that way. The times before when we had talked politics and culture and books, she had spoken with clear intentions, like someone who had read a lot of books and those books had gotten inside of her and stayed and helped form the true sentences that she spoke. She didn't speak that way to try to prove herself smarter than someone else. It was her love of language, a love of words. What we had seen on the river together would make you say things a lot worse than *bastards*. It could change your language, and the way you thought about some people. People who ran Transpower Inc.

When I pulled into the *Chronicle* parking lot, I saw Mickey's car. I parked and we got out and walked into the newsroom and to Mickey's desk. Mickey was talking on the telephone. Smoke was rising all around him from the cigarettes in the newsroom. He was standing up with the telephone squeezed against his left ear and shoulder while editing copy with a pencil.

"Don, I don't give a damn what that son-of-a-bitch said about me or my newspaper," Mickey said. "He's a piece of raw shit anyway. *Raw shit!* I'll talk to you later. We'll have a drink at Madeline's." Mickey hung up the telephone.

He turned to see Abby and me standing in front of his desk.

We were about to walk away and let Mickey finish his conversation.

"Maynard, what you got?"

"Mickey, Abby got some good shots. I think you'll like them. It was the same mess I saw yesterday on the river."

"I hope you like them, Mickey," Abby said. "What we saw is awful. Unbelievable even. They're destroying beauty on the river."

"Abby, I need these developed as quickly as you can and get them right back to me," Mickey said. "You got it?"

"Okay, Mickey. It won't take me long."

She left the newsroom with the two rolls of film and took the elevator to the third floor where the darkroom was and got to work.

"Nice damn job on the story, Maynard. Just a few changes I made. They were all minor. Keep it up. I like it. It read tight."

"Thanks, Mickey. I appreciate that."

I remembered what Mickey said after he had edited one of my first news stories for the *Chronicle* a few weeks after I was hired. I remembered then and always would.

"Maynard! This is a piece of shit! Re-write the whole damn thing and follow my corrections. Now, damn it, get it right this time."

Any new reporter could be verbally bashed the same way I was. Don't apply for the job if you're thin-skinned. Mickey's style could run you away from the paper, down Pine Avenue, across the river, and gone forever. But if you listened and learned and worked hard and began to understand Mickey, working for the paper could be a helluva a lot of fun. I had gotten better as a reporter and writer, and gotten better at understanding Mickey Burke.

"Now, I want you to follow up on this thing. No one knows where it's going. And there's a lot they aren't telling you. I want you to get back up there tomorrow and talk to folks on the river. And then I want you to stay in touch with the state and federal officials. I want to be able to tell our readers what's happening and why. You got it? This is your story. Yours alone."

"Yes, Mickey. I got it. I'll check in tomorrow morning before I go."

"No need. Get up and go. Just spend the day up there. Find out all you can. Talk to folks up there. The ones that have businesses connected to the lake and river. Property owners. See as many as you can. Get more quotes. More sources. Got it?"

"Okay."

"If these pictures are as good as Abby says they are, I'll ask Lucille if she might be available for some more work on your story. Her work upstairs has been pretty decent so far. I've read some of her stories. I've seen her art."

Lucille Webb was sixty-four and editor of the features section. She had started working at the paper when she was twenty-two, rare for a woman, especially in the South. During World War II, with many men serving overseas, Lucille had been the news editor, and a good one. When the war ended and the men returned, she returned to the features section. She married once and that was to the *Chronicle*. Still married to it. Abby liked working under her, but she wanted more than what that department could offer. She wanted what I had found in the newsroom.

"She would appreciate that Mickey. She's good."

I concealed my excitement for her and for myself, and the possibility of working more with her on the story.

"Well, we'll see. I think I can work it out. If her art's good, we'll use her again."

Mickey sat down in his desk chair, picked up the telephone, and made a couple of calls before dialing the darkroom. Thirty minutes later Abby was at his desk handing him the developed film.

"Here they are, Mickey. I think you'll like them. They look good."

"Thank you, Abby."

He took them fast without looking up at her. He was lighting another cigarette. Drinking more coffee.

My story had already been sent upstairs to the composing room where it was being laid out for tomorrow's paper. Mickey would decide which pictures from Abby to use with the story. He would send those up, too. This was the kind of thing that gave Mickey an even better high than what the martinis could do.

# Chapter 5

At six fifteen the next morning I was looking out my front window, waiting for the blue hatchback Mazda and the teenage boy who delivered my paper. I usually read the paper in the office, but on this day I didn't wait.

At six nineteen the paper hit my driveway with a *thump*. "It has landed," my dad said of newspaper deliveries. He had been a reader since he was a teenager. His appetite for the news and politics came from listening to President Franklin D. Roosevelt's radio broadcasts when he was a boy. Newspapers followed the radio for him. Sports page first, then the news. Later it was the other way around. His habit I acquired at about the same age. I walked out to get my paper shirtless and in boxer shorts. No one was looking but the mockingbirds and squirrels. They didn't seem to care. I picked up the paper and looked at it under a street light near my mailbox. I could easily see what I wanted to.

Mickey had placed the story on the front page above the fold with the picture of Tony and the dead fish. Abby's photograph was sharp, full of death, and as good as the others I had seen lately in the paper. Tony looked like a man capable of doing mean things to someone.

The story jumped to 8A and there was another of Abby's pictures. This one showed the dramatic change in the river's coloration because of the sickening effluent the company was discharging. Mickey added a third picture from the newspaper's library. It was a picture of the plant itself, and had been included in a press release mailed to the *Chronicle* three weeks before the plant had begun production. I wondered if the company now wanted the picture back. Bet they did.

The entire spread, with my by-line on page one, pleased me like no other story I had written for the paper. I took the newspaper inside and sat down on the sofa next to the record player that had a Flying Burrito Brothers' album on from the night before. I was not playing any music that morning. My roommate, Michael McLeod, who taught writing courses at Albany Junior College, had been long into last night with his girlfriend. He loved the desert harmonies of the Burrito Brothers. I read the story twice. Then a third time. I reread the lede and the final two paragraphs.

> CORDELE, Ga. - Officials from the state's Environmental Protection Division said they will begin testing samples of the Flint River to determine if a local company, Transpower Inc., is polluting the popular waterway by discharging its waste into the river.

I read the lede again before going through the rest of the paper, but was too excited to focus on and retain anything from the other stories. I folded the newspaper and placed it, with my story showing, on an end table next to a stack of albums.

"Well, Maynard, did you make the front page?" Michael said, as he walked into the den from his bedroom.

I was startled by Michael's voice, having gotten fixated on my thoughts and on the story. And about thinking of what was to come. It was unlike Michael to be up this early on a Saturday, but he had been thinking about my story, too.

He was a reader who liked equally the sentences of Ernest Hemingway and the lyrics of Bob Dylan. Michael was a bit over six feet tall, in excellent physical shape, and a tough basketball player. He wore his dark, black hair long and sometimes in a ponytail, and he usually kept a thick beard that he could grow in a few days. He played the guitar well, and looked like George Harrison, the former Beatle.

"Check it out. It's above the fold. Mickey played it out well."

Michael picked up the newspaper, sat down in a black vinyl chair that he had paid five dollars for at a garage sale, and began reading. I got up from where I was sitting, took a shower, put on faded jeans and a knit shirt, and took two notepads and two pens from my room before walking back into the den. Michael was about finished reading the story.

"Tonight the beers are on me, my man. Damn good story. Wish I had done it. We'll celebrate at Jim's Oyster Bar. Well done! You're going to be somebody someday, aren't you?"

"Thanks, man. Just trying to be me, that's all and nobody else."

"Hardest thing to do, they say."

"Maybe so."

"Helluva a story, my man."

"It played pretty well. Mickey and the rest of the guys at the paper did a fine job on the layout. It just looks damn good, doesn't it?"

"Any man that does that kind of work ought to drink free tonight."

"I agree with that. Can I quote you on that?"

"Quote me all you want. Beers on me tonight."

"You got it. I'm going back up to the river today and when I get home, I'll let you buy all you want. Put no restrictions on you. I believe a man should always do what he wants to do."

"That's a fine belief when it comes to beer. I'll see you then."

"See you."

It was early, but I left anyway. I drove slowly. It was a cool morning, but the heat would soon come. I was headed to Stripling's, a general store and diner near Lake Blackshear, to talk to locals about their river and what Transpower Inc. was doing to it. Mickey wanted a follow-up, and I did too. I hoped to meet the Saturday breakfast crowd over coffee and sausage and grits and eggs. It seemed like a good place to start.

My mind was clear and it went to Abby, then to Tony Patrick, to Lard Ass, and back to Abby again. It stayed with Abby most of the time. Then I thought about the death on the river, and the black water. The killing kind. The dying and dead animals I'd seen, and the ugliness of the water that killed them was fixed in my mind like a welded piece of steel. Sickening thoughts. The sun had come up dark orange and was sitting atop cornfields turning brown too early, hurting from the successive days of heat and little rain. There was little traffic on the highway. My mind was back to Abby when I arrived at Stripling's Diner.

Seven pickup trucks, mostly black and white ones, were parked outside of Stripling's near a neon sign that advertised a $3.99 breakfast and free coffee refills. I parked by the metal newspaper containers, and got out of my car and walked toward the diner and saw my story through the glass where the *Albany Chronicle* was being sold. There were only two copies left in the metal box. I hesitated a moment and looked again at the story and then went inside.

I walked to the counter and sat on a red vinyl stool and a waitress approached me wearing a blue apron over her dirty white blouse. Her gray hair was tied with a pink ribbon. She was trying to look pretty, but mostly looked tired. She was chewing gum rapidly, as if she was in a race and determined to win. She popped her gum like kernels of corn in a hot frying pan. On the left side of her apron, her nametag read "FLORA." Couldn't miss the name.

"Whatta you have, hun?"

I had just picked up the menu, had not read it, but ordered anyway.

"Give me a ham and cheese omelet, hash browns, water, coffee and cream. That's it."

She wrote on her order pad. Her pencil touched the paper for five seconds, looked like lines flying across the pad. I watched her do it.

"Okay, hun."

She turned and moved to another customer who had just sat down three seats away from me. Flora took that customer's order and returned to me and poured a cup of coffee leaving cream in a small, shiny tin pitcher. She left a glass of water in crushed ice for me.

"Your order will be up in a minute or two, hun. Won't take long. Hope you like the coffee. It's the best on the lake."

"Thanks. Looks good."

"It's always good, hun." She left to see another customer.

I began to drink the coffee and saw a uniformed law officer sitting in a nearby booth. He was a big man. Bigger, I thought, than Lard Ass. Wondered if he could contain a large alligator by sitting on top of it. Probably didn't teach that at the police academy. He had white, thick hair combed straight back and plastered with something that would've kept it immovable if he were outside during a hurricane. He was sitting with two other men in uniforms. They had badges and guns and had placed their hats on the table next to their coffee cups.

I thought about that man for a moment and realized I was looking at Crisp County Sheriff Sonny Dupree. I had seen his picture in the *Chronicle* a few times, and had met the sheriff once while covering the Watermelon Parade in Cordele. I had gotten a couple quotes from him that day to use in the story. Dupree had been on a float full of watermelons and ten pretty high school girls in shorts and tank tops all waving to the crowd lining Main Street. The local chamber of commerce called Cordele "The Watermelon Capital of the World." Maybe it was. The High Sheriff was having fun that day. He kept smiling and looking at the girls all around him, I remembered.

"Here's your food, hun. I hope you like it."

"Thanks, Flora. Looks real good."

She smiled at me and pushed a long strand of greasy hair behind her right ear and when she leaned over to wipe the counter with a white wet cloth next to me, the same strand of hair flopped over her eyes again. She pushed it back behind her ear again.

Flora looked sixty but could've been forty. Her brown eyes were streaked red as if her last restful night of sleep had been when she was a teenager. Or maybe she had never had one. She had the wrinkled hands of an old woman, and she had bitten and chewed most of her fingernails away.

Flora was about five feet six inches tall and if she weighed a hundred pounds, there would've had to been a couple hundred dollars' worth of quarters in her pockets. The Sheriff and his two deputies probably ate more that morning than Flora had eaten the previous month. She was a haggard little woman trying to keep smiling, yellow teeth and all. Busy that morning moving from customer to customer. I had eaten most of the omelet, when she returned.

"More coffee, hun?"

"Yes, Ma'm, please. I appreciate it. Food sure is good."

"Knew you'd like it."

"Yes, Ma'm."

She poured it fast, and I thought it would rise out of my cup and spill onto the counter. It didn't. She had poured thousands of cups of coffee. Didn't even need to look. Just needed to know the cup was empty. When she was about to walk away, I figured I ought to start with her. It was time.

"Flora, can I ask you a question?"

She pushed back her hair with her left hand, but it didn't make her look any better. She looked forever tired.

"Sure, hun, what's on your mind this morning? Some more food?"

"No, this is plenty. It's something else."

"What else, hun?"

"What are your customers saying about the fish kill? About what's happening to the river up here? What do they say about it? I've seen the river where it's a mess. Just awful."

She stood still and looked around at the people in the diner, and where the sheriff and his deputies were eating.

"Well, hun, lots of them are pretty upset, I reckon. They should be. Some of these good old boys have been saying some nasty things about that paper mill. Don't blame them one bit, I reckon. This here river and lake mean a lot to people 'round here."

"Has your business been hurt, Flora?"

I had pulled my notepad from my back pocket and a black pen from my front pocket. I flipped to the first clean page. Flora didn't notice what I had done because she was watching the sheriff and his deputies leave the diner, and other customers enter.

"Not that I can see. We still are busy around here. People got to eat, hun. You know what I mean?"

"Yes, Ma'm. I know what you mean."

Then she saw me write in my notepad.

"Who you with, hun? What do you want from me?"

"The *Albany Chronicle*. Don't worry, Flora. I won't quote you if you don't want me to. I'm doing a story on what's happening up here on the river."

"No, hun, keep me out of there. I've had this job for eleven years now. Longer than anything I've ever done in my life. I aim to keep it. I don't need to see my name anywhere but on this here name tag. You got that, hun?"

"Okay, Flora. You won't see your name in my paper. But I just want to take down a few things I can follow up on. I promise you I'll keep your name out of it."

"I guess I can trust you, hun. You look like an honest young man. You are, aren't you?"

"You can trust me, Flora."

"What's your name?"

"John Maynard. I have a story in today's paper about the river and Transpower Inc. I'm back up here to talk to folks like yourself about the problem. I want to know, my paper wants to know, what people are thinking, how they're feeling. The river's a mess right now. We all know that."

"Well, you go right ahead, hun. And do what you have to do. Talk to everybody you can."

She seemed relaxed now and convinced, I thought, that I wasn't going to quote her in a story. I changed my questioning to put her at ease.

"How often do the sheriff and his deputies come in here?"

"Almost every day, hun. You might as well call it Dupree County instead of Crisp County. He's been sheriff thirty years and his daddy was, too, for about that long. That's what I always heard, anyways. About his daddy."

"Flora, let me ask you…"

Before I finished my question, Flora was gone, having left me to wait on another customer sitting alone at the counter, four stools away. When she left, I turned around on my stool and saw that Dupree and his two deputies had stopped in the parking lot to talk with a black man who had just pulled into the diner in a white Lincoln Continental. The four men laughed, shook hands and departed. Dupree and his deputies got into their squad car and drove away. Dupree was behind the wheel. The black man came into the diner and sat at the counter.

During the 1960s, Dupree had arrested and jailed civil rights marchers in Crisp County, but by the mid-1970s he was hiring black deputies. Now when he campaigns, he speaks at black churches and attends their fish fries. Overtly he had changed to win at electoral politics. I remembered a recent story in the *Chronicle* when the state's General Assembly proclaimed Dupree Georgia's Lawman of the Year. The Crisp County Chamber of Commerce had a big banquet for him in Cordele. Lots of big shots were there, including executives from Transpower Inc. I knew one thing about Dupree for sure. He was a big man. He looked to be about five foot ten and around two hundred fifty pounds. I thought if Dupree and Lard Ass sat on an alligator together, that gator would never move again.

I paid Flora for the breakfast, tipped her, and left Stripling's and drove to Smoak Bridge, where a few fishermen were pulling their boats out of the water after bass fishing. By nine thirty it was already too hot for most fishermen. I parked, got out of my car, and met and talked to three fishermen about the polluted river and what might become of the lake. I got good quotes to use. I watched a party boat leave with two adults and six children and big rubber inner tubes and water skis, and I thought again about the awful smell of death just fifteen miles away. As the party boat got further away from the landing, I could still hear laughing children on the water.

I got back into my car and drove north past Stripling's and saw another sheriff's car, or maybe the same one from breakfast, parked in front of the diner. I slowed down and saw Sheriff Dupree walking out of the diner. Maybe he had come back for another sausage and biscuit. Or two more. The sheriff was carrying what looked like a newspaper. I drove on.

Five miles later and down a series of country roads where the land rolled with soybeans and peanuts, I stopped at Gentry's Country Store. Owner Willard Gentry was sixty-six, wore overalls every day, chewed Red Man tobacco, and spit into a rusted coffee can he kept on the counter. Sometimes he'd miss the can and tobacco juice would splatter on a customer. Most were too scared of him to complain. He wore a beat-up straw hat on top of his bald head and kept a red handkerchief in his front pocket next to his bag of Red Man.

He chewed first thing in the morning and the last thing at night. His father had owned the store during the Great Depression, and it never closed during those hungry times. Never made much money, but never closed. When his father died in 1950, Willard took over and had been behind the counter since. Willard, everybody in these parts said, "takes shit from no man."

Three men, all in overalls and wearing John Deere caps, were sitting on wooden benches outside of Willard's drinking Dr. Pepper in longneck bottles and sharing a large bag of pork rinds. They were children of the Great Depression and their weathered and tough hands had once kept mules steady plowing South Georgia's crimson soil. I talked to the men for several minutes, got some more usable quotes for my follow-up story. Then Willard Gentry came outside.

"Sir, my name's John Maynard, I'm with the *Albany Chronicle*. I'd like to talk with you a few minutes, if I could. Do you have time?"

"Son, you ask and I'll answer. I figure I know why you're here. It's 'bout those bastards ruinin' our river. If it's not, it should be."

"Yes, sir, it is. That's why I'm here. I want to talk about the river and what's happening to it."

"I'd like to shoot all them bastards. Or at least carve them up a bit with my catfish knife so their mommas wouldn't recognize them. Don't you think I should? Don't you think they deserve that?"

He had the knife strapped to his hip. Jim Bowie could have used it at the Alamo. It was that big.

"Yes, sir, I understand. I do understand how you feel."

"Well, maybe you do or maybe you don't, son. But I've been here all my life. Farmed this land with my daddy, who took me fishing on that river when I was a kid, and now I take my grandchildren there. They're going to mess around and end that for everybody. Those bastards. I swear to you, I may need to carve them up with this knife."

With his right hand, he grabbed the white handle of his knife, spit tobacco juice next to the red Coca-Cola machine. The spit would've killed a large insect, but it didn't hit one. I was taking notes now.

"Somebody needs to go to jail for a long, long time for doin' that to our river. And I reckon if they don't go to jail – I'll take care of them. You understand me, son? You hear me?"

He grinned and clutched his knife harder. And spit again.

"Yes, sir. I understand you. Has your business been hurt because of the dirty river and fish kill?"

"No, son, not yet, but I suppose it will be soon. You can almost smell that *shit* from here. It's just goin' to get worse until we shut those bastards down. Close the plant up if we have to."

"What about the folks who work there? What do you say about the good-paying jobs? People there make a good living. More money than they've ever made."

"You can't call it work, at least honest work, when what you're doing is destroyin' somebody else's work. Now can you son? Tell me, son, does that make good sense to you?"

"Nope, I guess you're right about that."

For the next twenty minutes, I kept writing and getting good quotes from Willard talking about the river, his family, and his long-standing ties to the land and its people. He was proud of his story.

"Mr. Gentry, I appreciate your time. Is there any final thing you want to say to me today?"

"Son, you just keep doin' what you're doin'. You never know what's on the end of a trotline. You can't see everything. But sooner or later you got to pull her up and when you do, you'll see it all. You'll see everything."

It was a quote I wouldn't use in the story but wrote it down anyway.

"Mr. Gentry, thanks again for everything. I appreciate you taking time to talk with me."

We shook hands, and I got in my car and left the store.

On the road again, the first car I passed was a sheriff's patrol car. It could've been the same one I saw at breakfast, but I wasn't certain. I saw three men in it. One had on a white hat or was it white hair? Then I saw a second patrol car stopped at a stop sign at a dirt road intersection. They didn't seem to be in a hurry to get anywhere.

"Those boys just don't have much to do around here," I said out loud.

I decided to drive unannounced to Tony Patrick's house, thinking on a Saturday afternoon he might not be working, but at home. I was right. I pulled into his driveway and parked next to *Cheap Sunglasses*. I got out of my car and walked through the opened garage and knocked on the door that led into the house. Tony answered.

"Well, well, good job this morning my famous reporter friend! It was a big front-page story for you. Well, at least I'm good for something, I reckon. Helpin' you get on the front page and all. You know you owe me for that."

"It played out pretty well. And Mickey sure liked it, Tony."

"Mickey who?"

"My editor, Mickey Burke."

"Hell, I liked it too. And that's more important than your editor. What brings you back to the shitty, polluted river today? They don't give you Saturdays off? You want to go see some more dead fish? Got thousands of them. All kinds of dead animals on the water."

"No, had enough of dead fish for a while. I've been talking to folks at Striplings, some fishermen at the lake, and then went over to Willard Gentry's place. I got some good quotes to use for a follow-up story."

"Yeah, I've known old Willard all my life. Before my daddy died of cancer a few years ago, he and Willard did a lot of fishin' together. Sometimes I went with them. He's not an ass licker. He don't take no shit. That's the thing about Willard I like most."

"I found that out. I did get some quotes from him I can use. Some that my editor would accept. Not the ones where he said he'd take his knife and carve up whoever's dumping the crap in your river."

"Yeah, that sounds like Willard. Good for you, Mr. Reporter. Glad you talked with him. He's a good man. Damn good man. Loves the river and the people here."

"What's next for you Tony? Have you had time to think it through?"

"I was on the phone last night and again this morning callin' folks about a meeting about what's happening up here. We've got to organize, John. It's got to be more than me. Hell, we'll call it Save the Flint Inc. I've been thinking about that name. What do you think? You like it?"

"Sounds like a winner. When will you meet?"

"I don't know. Maybe in the next two or three weeks. I'll let you know."

"I'll stay in touch with you," I said. "I want to see this through."

"I bet you will. You like the front page don't you?"

"It's not a bad place to be. Not that the other pages are bad."

"One other thing, John."

"What is it?"

"We're not goin' to let a bunch of rich, corporate assholes come in here and destroy the best thing about this place. I'm goin' to see this thing through, too. But I've got to have help, and I think I can get it. I'm willing to fight them if I have to. We *have* to organize. There's no other choice."

I was taking careful notes.

"One more thing, Tony. How many county deputies do you have up here?"

"Hell, I don't know. What's that got to do with that mess on the river?"

"I suppose nothing. But I sure saw several patrol cars this morning. They seemed to be everywhere I went. Almost like they were following me. Just curious."

"Maybe they were just trying to protect you from the bad guys."

"Maybe so, but it seemed odd."

"A lot of things are odd, John."

We talked for a few more minutes and Tony told me he was taking his sons on a boat ride that afternoon on Lake Blackshear. They would be in his pontoon or party boat, and he'd pull the boys in the water on big rubber inner tubes. His wife was going too.

"Tony, stay in touch and let me know about any meeting with Save the Flint."

"I will. When we meet, I want you there. Take care, John."

I left Tony's and didn't see any more Crisp County patrol cars on the way back to Albany.

# CHAPTER 6

I had decided to go by the newsroom, thinking Mickey might be there, as he occasionally was on Saturday afternoons when the Sunday paper was being put together. I wanted to tell him about my interviews and what I had for the follow-up story for next week.

I walked into the quiet office, always lightly staffed on Saturday. It was around two and Mickey wasn't there. I saw an opened pack of Marlboros on his desk and one burning down in his ashtray. Looked as if Mickey had been in, but slipped down to Madeline's to see the martini crowd.

I went to my desk and began writing the follow-up. The story came easy, just like the first one had. My lone typewriter was the only sound in the newsroom. I included interviews from the fishermen and Tony Patrick and a couple of good quotes from Willard Gentry and the men at his store. I read my notes about what Willard had said about never knowing what's on the end of a trotline, but didn't use it. A little more than an hour after I had begun the writing, I had almost completed the story. Then Mickey walked in.

"Maynard, what the hell are you doing here? You're off today. I thought so anyway. This is Saturday. Isn't it? What day is it?"

"Saturday."

"That's what I thought goddamnit."

"Mickey, I just got back from the lake and spoke to some folks about the situation up there. I think I've got a pretty good follow-up we can use."

Mickey was standing at my desk and picked up the pages I had written and read them. He took less than a minute, then put the pages back on my desk next to my typewriter.

"Good work, damn it, that's good. Keep at it. Who knows where the hell this thing is taking you. But go with it. Stay on those bastards. I like the quotes you got today."

"Thanks. I'll have it done in about thirty minutes."

"I'll use it Monday. Finish it, give it to me, and I'll go ahead and send it upstairs. I like the way it reads."

"Okay. Thanks."

Mickey walked to his desk, lit a Marlboro, sat down, kicked off his black leather shoes, and propped his bare feet on his desk, and made a phone call. He didn't like socks. I went back to work. About forty minutes later, I handed my copy to Mickey, who was on his third phone call since he had returned to the newsroom. He kept talking on the phone, but nodded and grinned at me as he took the copy. I nodded back.

I left the newsroom and went home. I wanted a cold beer and remembered Michael's offer from the morning. Michael was home when I arrived, and said the offer had not been withdrawn. He said there would be pitchers of beer and oysters for the page-one story. Can't argue with that.

Jim's Oyster Bar was off Pine Avenue near the railroad tracks and the Coca-Cola Bottling Co., a couple of miles west of the Flint River. It had opened the year I graduated from nearby Albany High School. Myself and several of my friends from school were part of the regular crowd in the beginning and still were. The bar was small and smoky from cigarettes, but the beer mugs always came with a thin coating of ice. They kept coming fresh with the pitchers. It was my favorite watering hole after summer leagues basketball games at the YMCA. Raw oysters, hot sauce, crackers, and cold beer.

When Michael and I walked into the bar, the jukebox was playing Lynyrd Skynyrd's "Sweet Home Alabama," and two college boys home for the summer were into their third pitcher of beer and singing along to the music. Two seats at the bar were open, and the dozen tables were already full. Some people were standing and drinking and talking. The cigarette smoke and the six o'clock Saturday crowd were settling in. We took the brown vinyl bar seats and Michael ordered a pitcher of beer. The bar maid brought the beer and two frosted mugs.

I saw a girl in the back of the bar and thought it was Abby. Her back was to me and when she turned, I realized it wasn't her.

After the first pitcher, Michael got up and went to the bathroom and I walked to the pay phone next to the foosball table. That was where the girl had been who reminded me of Abby. I put a quarter in the machine and dialed Abby's number. Saturday evening, I thought, she's out somewhere, probably on a date. Her phone rang twice and she answered.

"Hello."

"Hey, can you hear me, this music is loud!"

For the past twenty minutes The Doobie Brothers had been playing, including a song about love, called "South City Midnight Lady." I had heard clearly every word over the noise of the bar.

"Yeah, barely. Where are you?"

"I'm at Jim's with Michael."

"Did you go back to the river today?"

"Yeah, I did. Got some good interviews, wrote a follow-up this afternoon and gave it to Mickey. He's running the story Monday. It was a good day up there. Met several people."

"John, great story today."

"Hey, it had the best pictures in the paper. Who was that photographer anyway? I sure would like to meet her one day. Do you know who she is?"

"John, I was so excited when I saw the paper this morning and *my* name under those pictures. I just want to thank you for including me. Thank you so much."

"Well, I'm thanking you for working with me. Those pictures made the story."

"Easy, Johnny Boy. We know the truth. That was fine writing. Your words were all good. True words make true sentences."

"Thanks for saying that."

I paused and so did she. The Doobie Brothers kept singing. I saw Michael had returned to the bar and ordered another pitcher. He was talking to a blond-haired girl with a Led Zepplin T-shirt on. She was pretty. Had shorts on, not much material, and long legs that went all the way up to her ass. That's an old saying from my godfather. A smart man in many ways.

"Abby, come over tonight and we'll listen to some music. Do you have plans? I know I'm late asking, but I'd love to see you."

"No plans, Johnny Boy. What time?"

"An hour or so. How's that?"

"Perfect. What's your address?"

"Two fifteen North Cleveland. Not far from you."

"I know where you are. If you want I'll pick up a pizza," Abby said. "If you haven't eaten. How's that sound?"

"Sounds like a fine plan. I'll get some wine."

"Okay, I'll see you in a little bit."

"All right, Abby. Good bye."

"Bye John."

I hung up and walked back to the bar, but the blond was now in my seat.

"Where you been, Bro?" Michael said.

"I called Abby and she's coming by in about an hour. You think you can get me home and come back and see your friend?"

"Anything for my front-page man. Best wordsmith I know. Little Hemingway should be your new name."

"Easy with that."

Michael leaned an inch from the girl's right ear and whispered something. She smiled and nodded her head like a jack-in-the-box. Michael smiled back.

"Let's go, Hemingway. I'll get you home."

We left the blond and the music, and on the way home we stopped at a liquor store and I bought two bottles of merlot. I knew what she liked. After leaving the liquor store, Michael dropped me off at our house.

"Thanks, pal. I owe you," I said.

"You owe me nothing. Have fun. I'll see you sometime."

Michael left, heading back to the blond at Jim's Oyster Bar. I walked inside with the wine to wait on Abby.

I picked up newspapers and books scattered around the den, straightened a rug, got a handful of paper towels and dusted the top of the television and both end tables. It wasn't awful, I thought. I turned the television on to a Braves game and forty-five minutes later there was a knock at the door. I got up quickly to open it.

Abby was carrying a large pizza in a white box from Garganos, an Italian restaurant and her favorite, two blocks from my house. She was wearing white shorts, sandals, a tan blouse and smooth tanned legs. I wasn't thinking much about the pizza or wine or the Flint River or anything else. How could I?

"Hey, so good to see you, Abby."

"Likewise, Johnny Boy. Glad you called. I want to hear all about your day."

She came in and put the pizza on the coffee table next to where I'd put a bottle of merlot, two wine glasses, and a corkscrew. She sat down on the sofa and I poured the wine. We talked. We drank. And we talked some more.

I got up and put on a Van Morrison record and after a couple of songs we heard "Brown Eyed Girl."

"That's what I have sitting before me," I thought.

I poured us both a second glass of wine. In a little while I got up, walked into the kitchen and got two plates and paper towels. We ate pizza and kept talking and listening to one another and music we both liked.

"One of my dreams is to go to Ireland and see the land of Morrison and Yeats," Abby said. "I even think they look alike. I love the way they use words. I love them both, John."

"What about me?"

"Do I love you?"

"No, no, no, Abby, I didn't mean that. What about me? Can I go to Ireland with you? I'd like to see Morrison and Yates."

"Morrison maybe. Yates is long dead. Besides, you'll probably be stuck on the Flint River after all of this. Maybe even sitting on an alligator with Lard Ass. Who knows what's next for you, Johnny Boy."

"Maybe not, though. Any alligators in Ireland?"

"Yeah, just small ones. The kind that fit in your beer mug at an Irish pub."

"You know so many good things, Abby. Things most people don't know."

"All the important things. Here's another thing I know, Johnny Boy, I think big things are happening for you. Really big things."

Van Morrison kept singing and I was into her dark eyes and thinking about what it would be like with her in Dublin, the land of James Joyce. I had traveled there with a friend last summer. Wouldn't it be something to take her there, I thought? The land of the poets. Hell, I'd go anywhere with her. We leaned back on the sofa at the same time, eyes a little fuzzy from the wine. For a couple of minutes nothing was said. Nothing needed to be said.

After another song the album was over and I got up from the sofa to put another record on the turntable, opened the second bottle of wine, and poured two glasses. We drank those and talked some more about traveling, seeing everything worth seeing in this world. She said that's what she wanted.

"When do you want to go, Abby?"

"*Home? Now?*"

"No! Not home. To Ireland. To Ireland with me. When do you want to go?"

"Oh, Johnny Boy, there'll be time enough. I want to see and do it all. I want to travel, read, think, and write. And travel, read, think, and write. Do it all again. With you, if you like."

I put my arm around her and began kissing her, and we slid deep into the sofa. From the album *Blood on the Tracks,* Bob Dylan was singing "Tangled up in Blue." *Early one morning the sun was shining and I was laying in bed.* We both knew every word to the song. When she felt my touch around her shoulders, she pulled me closer and then I was gently on top of her. I kissed her, and she kissed back the same way, gentle and easy at first but then faster and harder with our mouths wide in expectation and pleasure. Another song played and she pulled away from me after a few moments, and I moved as she got up from the sofa, thinking that was it. Something was wrong. She had tasted and felt like no other. But this was over now, I thought. Then she took my right hand and led me to my bedroom. We stood next to my bed, and I undressed her and she did the same for me.

"Like I said, Johnny Boy, things are happening for you now. And for me, too."

"Yes, you did say that. Now I know what you mean."

"You feel so good to me right now. I love being with you, talking with you, listening to music with you. I love all of that."

She kissed me long again and stopped and looked at me in the dark.

"You're beautiful to me. You know that don't you? I love the same about you. I love to hear you talk, to hear your laugh. We're just the same."

I kissed both of her breasts tenderly and she held her head back as if she was reading a poem that had been written on my ceiling. I took her hand and led her to my bed.

I woke up around seven-thirty the next morning with Abby pressed against me naked and still asleep. I went into the kitchen, made some coffee, and walked outside to get the Sunday paper, and came back and poured myself a cup and began reading. She was still sleeping. I walked back into the bedroom and sat down at my desk with the coffee and looked at her. She was beautiful naked with a white sheet barely covering her breast and one leg completely uncovered. Her dark hair was spread over the white pillow. Her breathing was fluid and peaceful like she belonged here with me more than any other place in the world. Ireland even. She was sleeping on her left side facing a window where the sun's early rays were filtering in. I was sitting and watching all of her, and ten minutes passed. She woke up and looked at me looking at her.

"Are we in Dublin now, Johnny Boy? Has our train stopped already?"

"Yeah, we've been here awhile. I just had breakfast with Van Morrison. He wants to meet you. And Yeats is on his way, too. He has a new poem he wants you to read. Big things happening in Ireland, Abby."

"Please tell them to wait. I have something I need to do."

"What is it?"

She tossed the sheet from her, and I could see clearly now what

I couldn't in the dark last night. I got back in bed with her, and we made love again as the morning sun shone through the window. I held her close, her soft hair brushing against my face, her skin pressed against mine. It was a perfect fit. A few minutes passed, we barely moved. Then I spoke.

"You're not nervous about meeting Yeats and Morrison are you?"

"Should I be nervous?"

"No, not you, Abby. When they see you, you'll make *them* nervous."

The telephone rang.

I left Abby and walked into the den to answer it. A Sunday morning telephone call usually meant my parents. It would be an invitation from my mother for an afternoon meal or an offer to golf with my dad. Or both.

The call that morning wasn't from my parents. I picked up the telephone and said hello.

"Is this John Maynard with the *Albany Chronicle?*"

"Yes, this is John. Who's this?"

"John. This is Tony. Tony Patrick."

"Hey, man, how are you? I didn't recognize your voice."

"Well, I didn't either a few minutes ago."

"What do you mean by that? You didn't recognize your voice?"

"Let me ask you a question. Are your paperboys delivering rattlesnakes now days?"

"Tony, what in the hell are you talking about?"

"I'll tell you exactly what I'm talking about. I went out to get my paper, your paper, at around seven this morning and looked in the box marked *Albany Chronicle,* and it wasn't there. But a six-foot-long, dead, eastern diamondback rattlesnake was. Oh it's a pretty snake, John. But it didn't have a sports page. I about lost my voice then and almost shit in my pants. Do you know what I mean? Have you ever had a dead rattlesnake in your paper box?"

"No, I don't know what you mean, and I don't know if I believe you."

"I don't care if you don't believe me. It's true. It's damn true. You come up here and I'll give you this snake, and bring the Sunday paper when you come. 'Cause I damn sure don't have one."

For a few moments I thought it was a pretty good joke Tony was giving me. I had enjoyed his company, and he had an easy wit. A dead rattlesnake in your newspaper box would tend to make your voice unrecognizable, I thought, if that was the case. It seemed an odd time for Tony to call and try to be funny. Maybe it was not a joke.

"What are you going to do about it? Who you think would've done it?" I said.

"Let me go out in the yard where I buried that snake, dig him up, and ask him who killed him. And when I get the answer, I'll find that SOB, tell you his name, and beat the shit out of him. You can put that in your paper, Mr. Reporter."

"Tony, that could be my next story. 'Man Talks to Dead Snake and His Killer Identified.' "

"Yeah, that story should win some kind of shitty prize for you. You can bet on that."

"Seriously, Tony, who have you pissed off up there?"

"If you'd asked me that ten years ago, I would've said five or six girls and an equal number of cops."

"It's not ten years ago. It's now."

"Well, no shit buddyro. You big-time reporters are *really* on the ball. Hell, how should I know who puts dead rattlesnakes in a newspaper box? I do know *now is now*. You figure this one out."

"You think this is about Transpower and what you said about them polluting the Flint? Is that the connection you're making? You think this is somebody's response to our story?"

"Yeah, maybe it was that PR prick with the company. What's the prick's name? Harris, or something like that. Yeah, that's it, Harris. He's a real piece of work. Every time he talks a turd falls out of his mouth. I might as well call the plant manager. Good old Mr. George Woodson. What was his quote in the paper? Oh, yeah, 'We at Transpower put the environment first.' I believe I'll call both of them right now and ask them both over for Sunday dinner. Maybe I'll cook them some fresh, polluted, sick catfish from the river. Or I can cook this rattlesnake they left me. What do you think?"

"Tony, public relations pricks aren't usually trained that way. Not the ones I've been around anyway."

"Well, Reporter Man, you figure it out and call me when you do. I got to go talk to my dead snake. He's feeling kind of lonely out there by himself."

"All right, Tony, thanks for calling. I'll be in touch."

I hung up the telephone and returned to my bedroom where Abby had gotten up, put her clothes on, and made my bed.

"Who called you? James Joyce? Does he have a new short story he wants us to read?"

"No."

"It must have been Yeats. What's the news from Ireland this morning?"

"It wasn't Yeats. It wasn't Joyce. It was Tony Patrick, and he's got a problem. Instead of the *Albany Chronicle* this morning, he found a dead rattlesnake in his newspaper box in front of his house. A big one, too, he said."

"A dead *rattlesnake*? You sure he wasn't joking?"

"No, Tony was serious. It's no joke. Well, it's one helluva sick joke, I guess."

# CHAPTER 7

Monday morning in the office I read my follow-up story on page 2A and got a call from Tony, who said he was organizing a meeting at the Opry Barn near Lake Blackshear, and inviting anyone interested in "saving the Flint." The meeting would be in two weeks and Tony wanted me to announce the event in the *Chronicle*. I took notes over the phone and when we hung up, I started typing.

The Opry Barn, a place for country music shows and farm conventions, was three miles south of the lake and would accommodate about a thousand people. Tony was hoping to fill it. During our telephone conversation he used the phrase "power to the people" four times, and I found a place for it in the press release. Maybe it should be "power to rattlesnakes," I thought.

I walked to Mickey's desk and gave him the story, about three hundred words, about the upcoming meeting and Tony's efforts to organize a group he was calling Save the Flint Inc. Mickey told me to cover the event at the Opry Barn, but he knew he didn't have to.

"Stay with the story wherever it takes you. Damn good job so far. Stay with it, Maynard."

"Thanks, Mickey."

The press release would run the next day, Mickey said, and then a shorter version the day before the meeting. I told Mickey about the rattlesnake.

"Maynard, your boy up there on the lake and our paper have pissed somebody off. A dead snake won't hurt anybody, but somebody had to find that snake and kill it before they put it in his paper box. Somebody's serious."

"Do you think it was somebody with the company? Somebody

with Transpower?" I said.

"Makes sense doesn't it? Your source, hell, our paper, probably pissed them all off. Don't worry about it, goddamnit. You just stay on the story. The public has a right to know if a company's destroying a river. Don't you think?"

"Sure the public should know, but I'm worried about Tony. Mickey, that's just a sick thing for anybody to do. To put a dead snake in a man's paper box."

"Has your man up there pissed anyone else off besides Transpower?"

"He said no. But he did say that some years ago he had pissed off a few girls and a few cops. Back before he got married and had children."

"Well, goddamnit, there's no news there. You aren't certain, and maybe never will be, about what's in his past and what he does with his time today. *All* of his time. Maybe he's selling drugs and pissed off a client. Who knows? Who really knows about anyone, Maynard, you understand what I'm saying?"

"Yeah, Mickey. I know what you mean. Maybe he got into a fight at the Gator Pit and whipped the ass of a good old boy. Who knows?"

"Or maybe one of those pulp heads working for Transpower, making three times as much money as he ever had, took offense to Tony and our story. Your story, Maynard."

"That's possible, I guess."

Mickey picked up the telephone to make a call, and I walked back to my desk. My phone rang, and it was Tony Patrick.

Tony had called me from his Cordele real estate office and said all four tires on his truck had been slashed. They were as flat as the head of the dead rattlesnake that he had found in his newspaper box. Whoever had cut his tires walked to the back of his office where his parking lot was enclosed by four large oak trees strung with Spanish moss. From the office it's difficult to see what's happening in the parking lot, he said. Tony had been in the office about thirty minutes before heading to his truck to meet a client. That's when he saw what had happened to his truck. Tony never worried about anything like that happening before this morning. From now on, he would have to.

"I'm having a run of bad luck up here, John. No, I think it may be worse than that."

"I think you're right. Somebody's real pissed at you, Tony. This is a bad pattern developing."

"Well, you're a real genius to figure that out. You reporters are *smart*. Hell, yeah, somebody's pissed at me, but if I get my hands on whoever's doing this shit, it'll be worse on them."

"What are you going to do now, Tony?"

"Nothing. Other than go buy four new tires. They screwed me good this time."

"Who screwed you?"

"Who do you think? Who've I pissed off? You know the answer, Mr. Reporter. Why do you have to ask that question? You know damn good and well who I've pissed off up here. You pissed them off too. You better be careful."

"You mean Transpower?"

"Hell, yeah. Transpower! Transcrewed!"

"Just be careful."

"You too."

After the call ended I thought for a few moments about the dead rattlesnake and slashed tires. This was something more than a run of "bad luck," as one of my college roommates once said when he flunked two classes, wrecked his car, and caught his girlfriend screwing one of his fraternity brothers, all in the same week.

"They play hardball out there," my roommate said.

What was happening to Tony had nothing to do with luck. I leaned back in my chair and picked up a pencil I used to correct typed copy. I tapped the pencil repeatedly on the desk and thought about my first boat ride with Tony in *Cheap Sunglasses*. Going down the river that day with Tony was beginning to seem like a long time ago. Whoever was doing this to Tony was playing hardball, too.

Over the next week or so I continued to handle minor assignments from Mickey, re-writing press releases and covering politicians who spoke at the Exchange Club and the Rotary Club, but the whole time I did these things my mind was on the river and Tony. It stayed on Abby, too. I continued to pursue the river story.

I wrote another story, this time quoting a biologist from the University of Florida and researchers from the University of Georgia about the damage that untreated waste from paper mills can do, and will do to plant and animal life. I had seen and smelled the damage up close. I conducted the interviews by phone and Mickey played the story on 2A on a Friday.

Three days later another story I wrote appeared, indicating that state lawmakers representing Albany and the Lake Blackshear area were forming a committee to study the pollution problem and how to stop it. I used five sources for the piece and all were elected lawmakers. Mickey put it on the front page. The next day I got a call from Lard Ass at the Gator Pit.

"Did you hear about it yet? Have you heard?"

"Heard what? Lard, what are you talking about?"

"About your new buddy, good buddy. Did you hear what happened?"

"Who? Lard, what the hell you talking about? Tell me what's going on."

"Did you hear what happened to Tony? I just thought you'd know by now. Hell, you know everything else, don't you?"

"What happened to him, Lard? Is he all right? What's going on?"

"They got him. Somebody got him comin' out of my place last night. They got him good, but it was bad. It was *real* bad. Feed a monkey and watch him shit. It was bad."

"Who are they? What's going on?"

"Hell fire. I don't know, maybe it's the rattlesnake people. Maybe it's the tire people. They're on his ass like a catfish on chicken gizzard. Poor Tony. Feed a monkey, watch him shit."

"Is he okay? Just tell me. Is he okay?"

"Well, hell fire, he's going be all right. He's mighty beat up, though. Mighty beat up. They bloodied 'im up."

Then Lard told me what happened. Thirty minutes before sundown yesterday, Tony had come to the Gator Pit to remind Lard and the few customers there of the upcoming organizational meeting of

Save the Flint Inc. at the Opry Barn. Tony stayed about an hour or so, had a couple of beers and told Lard he'd see him in a few days at the meeting. He'd brought pamphlets about the meeting and gave them to Lard, and left the Gator Pit. Lard thought he had left. That's when they got him.

When Tony walked out the front door of the Gator Pit only Lard was inside and about to close for the evening. It had been another day in which his cash register had opened only a few times. It was dark, hot, and there were stars in the clear night sky that Tony would've usually stopped and looked at and enjoyed for a few moments. He had done that kind of thing since his dad had taken him camping when he was two.

Tony kept walking toward his truck, but never made it there.

As Tony passed the picnic table near the dock and the water oak trees, two men in black masks approached him. They had been hiding behind his truck. One of the men grabbed both of Tony's arms and twisted them behind his back. Tony groaned and twisted hard, but it didn't help. The one that had Tony was a big, powerful man with a grip that would only end when he wanted it to. Tony could do nothing. The second man kicked him in the groin. Tony moaned again. The one who kicked Tony then hit him five times across the face and head with a thick piece of wood. Nothing was said.

The big, powerful man released Tony and he dropped to the ground. He was hurt. The two men disappeared. All of it took less than a minute, the way Tony remembered it. Lard figured about the same.

Five minutes after Tony walked out of the Gator Pit to go home, Lard did the same, locking the business for the night. That's when he heard the moans.

Tony's eyes were swelling black and blood was streaming from his nose and chin, covering his white University of Georgia T-shirt. Lard half-carried Tony to the picnic table where he sat down to breathe again and to try to think clearly again. Lard ran back into his store to put crushed ice in a plastic bag and get a wet cloth. He returned and gave the bag to Tony, who placed it on his head, his pounding head. Lard took the wet cloth and wiped the blood from Tony's face.

After four or five minutes, the bleeding stopped. The pain didn't, and wouldn't for hours.

"Now you know everything I do. Feed a monkey, watch him shit. Mr. Reporter Man, I thought you would've found out by now. Thought you knew everything."

"No, I didn't know. Did he get stitched up? Did he see a doctor?"

"I don't think he did. If they had hit him any more he would've ended up in the hospital. That's the way I got it figured."

"I'm going to call him now, Lard. Thanks for calling me."

"Okay, good buddy. That's some monkey shit up here. All you can do is feed the monkey and watch him shit. That's all. You take care, good buddy. I hope they don't get you. Feed a monkey and watch him shit. Take care, good buddy."

"You too, Lard."

Then I called Tony's house.

"Hello."

"Tony, I just talked to Lard and he told me what happened to you last night at his place. What's happening up there? Are you okay?"

"It does make a man miss his dead rattlesnake and cut tires. Boy, those were the good old days, weren't they? Now this shit. Yeah, man, I'm fine, but my head's still killin' me. They worked me over pretty good. I sure hope they come back and see me."

"Tony, this isn't funny anymore."

"Well, no shit. It never was. I'm the one getting the hell beat out of him. I stopped laughing some time ago, Mr. Reporter. Don't you know?"

"What are you going to do about it?"

"Nothing for now. What can I do?"

"Did you get a description of the guys who did it?"

"Only that they were big and strong. And they hurt me."

"You got to do something. At least report it to the sheriff's office."

"That won't do any good. I have no description to give them. I know one thing, I'll have to wear sunglasses for the next few days. I look like I belong in a freak show. They got me good, whoever it was."

"Man, you got to look out for yourself. It's getting dangerous up there."

"*Getting* dangerous? Hell, it already is for me."

# CHAPTER 8

*When the four riders appeared in the meadow, Lady Marion was serving the orphans bread and meat with the village priest, who thanked God for the food before they began their meal. She saw them in the distance, but she smiled and handed each child a plate of food anyway. She folded her soft white hands in prayer and the twelve children did the same.*

*The riders came faster now, with their horses kicking up grass and dirt as they approached her, the padre, and the children. The four horsemen removed their swords from their sheaths and held them high. The children screamed as they saw what was coming. The padre knelt and said a Hail Mary. Then another one.*

*Lady Marion stood over the children, pulling them all next to her. The riders were closer now. Close enough to see their dirty beards and the saliva from their horses. The children screamed louder.*

*The arrows came quickly from a bluff nearby. One, two, three, four. All the riders were hit and fell.*

Then I awoke from the dream.

I had been having dreams like that since Abby and I slept together. Dreams about a dark-haired woman, strong and resolute, but who was sometimes in danger and in need of rescue. Each dream was an affirmation that Abby was in both my visible and invisible worlds. That was what I told myself. I had fallen asleep on the sofa that Saturday afternoon while reading Ernest Hemingway's *A Farewell To Arms*.

That evening Abby was assigned to cover the annual Debutante

Ball, and take pictures at Pine Valley Country Club. We talked a few minutes on the telephone and agreed to meet for drinks at Yesterday's after her assignment.

"Yeah, Johnny Boy, I am going to be with the Blue Bloods tonight. God's *real* chosen people. They are so blessed and the rest of us are so not blessed. I can't wait to see all their fake smiles and hear their fake words. Oh, the fakeness of it all."

"Be polite now, Abby."

"I'm not worthy, John. You know I grew up in a doublewide. I guess my parents didn't love me like the parents of the Blue Bloods. How could they ever love me, making me live in a trailer? I'm not worthy to be around those debutantes. God's chosen flock, John."

"Yeah, yeah, I've heard it all before. Poor, poor Abby."

"John, God has blessed the rich. Don't you know? It's in the Bible. Says so in the Sermon on the Mount."

"Like I said, try to be nice when you get out there."

"Oh, I will. I promise, I'll genuflect at their altar. And I'll say nice things about all those rich daddies and their perfect children. You and I are just part of the great unwashed, Johnny Boy. The great unwashed."

We laughed, and I knew how Abby wanted something more from journalism than writing about Albany's debutantes. She wanted "real news stories," as she had told me many times. She wanted something that mattered, something that made a difference in peoples' lives. I wanted the same for her.

"Do your best tonight," I said.

"Oh, I will. I'll do my best not to tell them how I actually feel. I'll see you later at Yesterday's."

"Looking forward to seeing you."

"Goodbye, John."

"Bye."

Later that evening I got to Yesterday's before Abby and took the same table we had used after my first river-trip with Tony. It was there I had told her about the things I had seen that day. I was thinking about her and how she loved a good story properly told, and how much I liked the sound of her laugh and the touch of her hands on me.

The waiter came and lit the tall white candle and I ordered a beer. A few minutes later he returned with the beer and put it on a red and white coaster. I told him thanks and I wanted to start a tab, and that I was expecting someone in the next few minutes. There were tables available and spaces to drink at the bar. It was slow. That was fine with me. I waited and drank my beer.

I was almost finished when I saw her come up the stairs. She looked in my direction and I stuck my right hand up in the air. She smiled at me and came over to our table.

Her hair was shorter than Lady Marion's, but prettier. Their dark eyes were identical.

"Good to see you tonight, Abby. You look great."

I got up and hugged her and pulled her chair out for her. She was wearing a green-flowery sundress that showed her tanned, athletic legs and bust line. She had been in her high school and college marching bands, and played softball on a church team. She was more beautiful than any debutante.

"Here we are again, Johnny Boy. You got our old table and all along I didn't think you were a romantic. Well, I guess I was wrong. I guess a girl can learn something new every day."

"I wanted to sit at the bar, but the owner said he'd throw me out if I didn't take this table. It's the only reason I got it."

"Funny, Johnny Boy. Funny. Very funny."

The waiter came back and we both ordered beers, and the talking began. Music, books, poetry, Tony Patrick and the river, her family, my family, even bitching about the debutants.

"Were you nice to all the perfect rich girls at the country club?"

"Sure, John. It's not often you get to be around human perfection. I did celebrate it. I'm just so lucky to get that assignment. Flawless people, all of them. Perfect teeth, perfect hair, and daddy's fat checkbook. Blessed by God, Johnny Boy. Blessed by God Almighty."

"I hope you were nice."

"Enough about the debutantes, when are we going to Ireland?"

"Soon, Lady Marion, soon. Real soon."

"Oh, now I got a new name for our trip. And I suppose you're Robin Hood?"

I told her about my dream that afternoon, and others I'd had recently about a woman, a woman I cared for and loved and one who needed my help. A beautiful woman with dark hair and soft skin.

"I don't mind being saved by you, Sir John. But only by you."

The talking and beers continued there, and then at Abby's apartment.

The next morning at her apartment she made coffee and scrambled eggs, light and fluffy. Abby cooked while wearing only an extra-large T-shirt with Disney World emblazoned on the front. Much of her legs were in full view, and when I looked at them in the kitchen I was reminded of how good they felt wrapped around me the night before. We made love twice that night and once in the morning. We kept talking. She made grits and toast, and put plenty of butter on each.

White shelves in her den contained lots of books and she said, "They're a good start, but the road is long." Hemingway, Fitzgerald, and Twain were some of her favorite novelists. They were all there. Yeats, Rimbaud, Frost and Bob Dylan and Van Morrison were some of her favorite poets. She had poets on paper and on vinyl stacked by her turntable. Some had spoken to us that night before our lovemaking began. The den and the books had the feel of a place where old friends have come, talked, laughed, and were slow to leave. It all felt right to me.

"Was that one of your heroic dreams last night, Sir John?"

She placed a plate of food before me at her kitchen table with a shiny glass top and four black iron chairs.

"What? What are you talking about?"

"Oh, Johnny don't be coy with me."

"Coy? I had a college roommate named Roy. I don't know anyone named Coy. Do you? That's an odd name."

She laughed as she sat down in a chair at the table and took a sip of coffee and picked up a fork. We began eating.

"Not only do you fire your arrows straight and kill the bad guys, you're some medieval comedian. You'd make a great court jester. Maybe you could write jokes for King Arthur one day. That'd be a great job, wouldn't it?"

"Abby, I really don't know what you're talking about. Who is this *Coy* guy? Someone you used to date?"

"Lady Marion wants to know if what happened last night was a dream. Was it real or a dream? What was it?"

"Of course it was a dream. Everything is a dream. But some dreams do come true, Abby."

Over the next few days at work I kept in contact with most of my sources who had helped me with the Flint River story, and wrote a couple of follow-up pieces using quotes from the state's Environmental Protection Division, state politicians, and Eugene Harris, Transpower's public relations "turd" as Tony Patrick called him. The EPD had begun testing the water for pollutants. It would be a few weeks before any results were released to the media. Other news outlets were now covering the story. Even the *Atlanta Constitution* and television stations in Atlanta.

"The river is just low now and when it returns to its normal level, normal coloration of the water will return. By this fall everything here will be back to normal," Harris said. The same thing he had said earlier.

I was able to get plant manager George Woodson again on the telephone, and his quotes were a replica of Harris's.

"It's just low water flow right now in the river. When the rains come, it will all be back to normal. Everything will be back to normal."

Tony had called me on a Wednesday to remind me of the upcoming organizational meeting of Save the Flint Inc. at the Opry Barn a few miles from Lake Blackshear. The meeting was scheduled for the following Friday evening at seven, and Mickey had arranged for Abby to go with me to photograph it. Tony expected a big, "pissed off crowd that had been pissed on," he said. It was an accurate prediction.

In spite of the dead rattlesnake, slashed tires, and the beating Tony had suffered that night at the Gator Pit, he had not folded. He had not quit. His eyes and his face had returned to normal, the swelling and blackness from the blows had disappeared. He wasn't sure when his life would become normal again, but his face was. He had taken hours and hours away from his family and real estate business the last few weeks since becoming committed to fighting the company's "blind parrots," as he called Harris and Woodson.

"Those two sumbitches don't care about nothin' but goddamned money," Tony said. "It's sickening when I think long about it. Nothing but money matters to them."

Tony had worked hard using newspapers and radio stations to advertise the meeting at the Opry Barn. He mailed postcards with an aerial picture of the river taken by one of his crop-duster friends. The photograph showed the natural brown color of the Flint, but at the company's discharge pipe, and covering one half of the river's width for a few miles, the river was as black as oil fresh out of the earth. Black as the blackest coffee at Stripling's Diner. That picture had become a powerful tool that Tony was using to promote the meeting, and it seemed to be working.

It was a tragic, clear reminder of what was happening to the waterway. For folks who loved the river and lake and used it to boat, swim, and fish, that photograph made their stomachs tighten. It made them angry. Those were the kind of folks who would be at the Opry Barn. This meeting, as Tony saw things, was the beginning, and he was prepared to call others throughout the summer, for the rest of the year and beyond in efforts to pressure Transpower and state and federal politicians to stop the company from dumping waste into the river. Tony was digging in and hoping others would join him in the fight. I admired that about Tony, or any man who took a stand against long odds over something he felt inside, deep inside. If that man turns out to be wrong then in the end, he needs to own up to it. I never doubted Tony was right to do what he was doing. I had seen and smelled the river up close.

"He don't take no shit." That was the ultimate compliment my dad could give another man. I was certain that if Dad ever met Tony, that's what he'd say about him. Tony had said the same about Willard Gentry.

Now when I thought about Tony and all he had been through

and what might happen as he continued to push back against the company, I remembered my father's phrase. It fit. I was thankful that my mother and father were the way they were, and hoped they would be around for a long time. I hoped the same for Tony.

The day of the Opry Barn meeting, I picked Abby up around six that evening. My dreams had remained vivid, and last night I dreamed I was hiking alone on top of Blood Mountain in North Georgia when a woman in the distance began crying out for help. I ran and tried to get to her, but slipped on a root and fell and hurt my leg. I never made it to her, but heard her cries grow louder and louder. I didn't tell Abby about that dream.

I drove slowly across town under giant live oak trees with Spanish moss lining the avenues and parked in front of her apartment. Seconds after I rang her doorbell she appeared with her camera and notepad, and the smile that I had been missing that day.

"Are you ready?" I said.

"Do I look ready?"

"You look perfect."

"Let's go then."

The day was still hot, but soon the sun would begin to set. I drove out of her parking lot toward the river and the people angry about what was happening on it. This was Tony's big night.

# CHAPTER 9

At six forty-five we arrived at the Opry Barn and saw its two large parking lots full of cars and trucks, and that Tony Patrick was probably right in that a thousand people would attend.

I counted at least a dozen tractors and two Crisp County Sheriff's patrol cars, with a deputy in each. The lawmen looked to be eating and drinking something from large Styrofoam cups. I thought they looked like the same two I had seen at Stripling's Diner some weeks earlier with Sheriff Sonny Dupree, but couldn't be certain.

I parked near Highway 300 next to a row of tall, green cedar trees planted in a neat line along the entrance to the parking lot. Abby and I got out and walked together and saw Tony standing by the front doors at the Opry Barn. He had been there since six fifteen greeting folks as they came, as would a high school football coach charging his players before the homecoming game. People up here had known and respected Tony and his family for many years. They had found the right leader.

"It looks like a great turnout for you," I said, extending my hand to shake his.

I looked at Tony's face to see if the hurt was still there from the attack at the Gator Pit. Tony's face had healed nicely.

"I haven't seen that prick PR man, Harris, from Transpower. I've been waiting on him and George Woodson. I know they're coming. I sent flyers to their houses."

"I doubt you will see Harris and his plant manager," I said.

"You never know what might happen. There've been a lot of surprises lately. Don't count them out."

"Hello again, Tony," Abby said, now extending her hand to Tony.

"Well, good to see you again, Abby. Thanks for coming, and thanks for all your work up here. You and your Big Shot Reporter boyfriend are going to be famous one day. One day soon. I'm going make both of you famous. I might not be alive to see it, though."

"Now Tony don't talk like that," I said. "I don't want to hear that, neither does Abby."

"Yeah, Tony, we'll leave the fame to you," Abby said. "We just want to tell the story."

"That's not for me either," Tony said. "Fame,, that is. I never wanted any of this."

Tony tilted his head toward the Opry Barn, where more than a thousand people were waiting for him. Standing room only and about a hundred folks along the walls on both sides and the back. "But let's go in and get this damn thing started."

Tony began the meeting by thanking everyone who had come and said this was the beginning. He used the phrase "power to the people" twice. "All of us here must be committed and united. We are going against a powerful multi-billion dollar corporation that appears to be destroying our river. We have to be willing to fight back." The crowd cheered and clapped and hollered as if they were at a high school homecoming game. He discussed his plans for the next few months, including efforts to raise money and hire attorneys for possible legal action against the company. Louder cheers followed. Abby took pictures of Tony at the podium and others who followed him.

One of the other speakers was Dr. Robert Langston, a biologist from Florida State University, who I had spoken to over the telephone for one of my follow-up stories about the polluted river. Langston was a nationwide expert on damage a pulp mill can do by discharging its waste into a river system. He had been studying and documenting the consequences of such action for almost twenty years. Langston had driven three hours from Tallahassee to attend the meeting. I was eager to hear what he would say publicly.

Ten years ago he predicted correctly that Transpower's pulp plant on the Fenholloway River in Florida would have a long-term "destructive impact" on that eco-system. The fisheries and water quality there had yet to return to what they were before that plant began production. Those at the Opry Barn got a slideshow from the fish kill that occurred on the Fenholloway years ago. It looked like the Flint River to them. Watching the slides made the crowd angrier.

"The company's ten million gallons of waste that's being dumped daily into the Flint is basically composed of sodium sulfate extracted from pine trees as they are turned into pulp," Langston said. "Those chemicals, in high concentrations, can be devastating on animal life and water quality."

Many in the crowd for the past few weeks had seen and smelled the results of that discharge. There was silence when he spoke.

After Langston's presentation, Dr. Ralph Caldwell, a family physician from nearby Americus who had owned a house on Lake Blackshear for fifteen years, had a slide presentation of his own. He had taken a boat ride past the company's discharge pipe on the Flint and saw what I had seen with Tony.

Ralph Caldwell documented what he saw and had a sharp eye with the camera. There were hundreds of dead mussels, which were food for fish and raccoons and other animal life. He showed pictures of dead fish by the hundreds, and dead ducks and turtles. Same as Abby and I had seen.

"Boo! Boo! The hell with those bastards at the mill! The hell with all of them!" hollered a man wearing overalls and a wide-brimmed straw hat. He was sitting in the second row behind Abby and me. He stood up unannounced, not needing a microphone to be heard.

"I feel the same way," Ralph Caldwell said.

The crowd clapped and cheered for several moments.

"These people are pissed," I said.

"They should be," Abby said. "They have every right to be. A lot of them have seen what we've seen."

"I mean *really* pissed."

"Do you blame them?"

"No."

When the crowd subsided, the doctor from Americus spoke again.

"The company, and even our own state environmental folks, have repeatedly said the river's discoloration and odor is not polluting our river and lake…" Dr. Caldwell said, but was interrupted.

"*BULLSHIT! IT'S ALL BULLSHIT!*" hollered a man from the back of the Opry Barn. "LET'S MAKE THE BASTARDS LEAVE! LET'S SHUT DOWN THE DAMN PLANT!

The crowd erupted again with loud clapping and cheering and some shrill whistling. It took them a couple of minutes to calm down before Dr. Caldwell could complete his remarks. He was a patient man. There were a few other speakers after Caldwell. They were landowners along the river and lake, and fishermen who had caught bass, bluegill, and catfish for years on the river and now were unable to do so south of Transpower and its discharge pipes. The beauty they once enjoyed was disappearing. After Caldwell completed his presentation, Tony Patrick returned to the podium to close the meeting.

"Without good clean water for ourselves, our children, and their children, we lose a part of who we are and the beauty of this area. It would be shameful to allow this to happen. We're going to fight it. The river belongs to the people. To us. And we must preserve it and protect it for our children and their children. It doesn't belong to Transpower. It doesn't belong to any corporation no matter how much money they have. We'll shut them down if we have to." Tony said, causing the crowd to erupt again before he completed his final statement.

When the cheering ended he closed the meeting, reminding everyone to leave their names, phone numbers, and addresses on the forms he had placed on tables at the entrance of the Opry Barn. There'd be future meetings, he said, and a "plan of action" about how to proceed, and he needed everyone at the Opry Barn that night to help. He repeated that line.

"Power to the people! Power to the people!" Tony said, amid more cheers. It reminded me of what I had read about demonstrations in the 1960s against the Vietnam War and in support of civil rights for blacks. A movement of people for something bigger than themselves. Abby and I were part of something we had not experienced before as reporters. This, I thought, as Tony left the podium and the meeting ended, was why I had wanted to become a reporter all along. Same thing for Abby.

After the meeting, I waited to speak with the Florida State biologist, Robert Langston, to learn more about what his future role might be in all of this. It was something that Mickey Burke had always told me.

"Now, goddamnit Maynard, you'll get your best quotes one-on-one. Always talk to your sources that way. All of them. After the speeches have been made and everyone else has left, you see them one-on-one. You got it?"

"I got it, Mickey."

"Good. Don't forget it."

It had always been good advice. With the crowd filing out of the Opry Barn, Abby and I walked on the stage together and behind the podium near the row of chairs that the presenters had used before coming to the microphone. Langston was still there. He wore a brown, wide-brimmed cowboy hat and tan boots that needed polishing. He was a little shy of six feet tall and had a brown, thick mustache, and sideburns that looked like they belonged to singer Neil Young. Langston looked to be in his mid-forties, and he had spoken clearly during his presentation, making the scientific aspect of this story easy to understand. He had an easy demeanor and probably was a fine classroom teacher.

Tony was on stage talking to Dr. Caldwell from Americus and some other men and women who had been part of the crowd. Abby began taking more pictures as I asked the biologist if he would answer a few follow-up questions. He agreed.

"Rivers can be restored to some degree. But not until what is being dumped into them is put somewhere else or greatly diluted," Langston said. "Once an industry gets on a river and does these things, it can take years to repair the damage. Pulp mill waste has a history of doing terrible things to the natural environment."

"What's your role going going to be in all of this in the weeks ahead?" I said.

"Nothing permanent yet. But Tony has informed me that he had a discussion with a member of the Crisp County Power Commission, they have had a plant on the lake for years, and they may consider hiring me as consultant. I would welcome that, if it occurs."

"If it happens, how would that work?"

"I would suggest an extensive long-term study at this point to see what the consequences of all this might be. I'd be willing to help, but it's up to them and the folks here tonight. They need data. Scientific data."

"Can these folks here tonight win?"

"What do you mean by win? It's always a hard, hard struggle. These companies will fight hard. These corporations are powerful and money speaks louder than fish, birds, beautiful water, and everything these folks here tonight appreciate about their river and lake. It's unfortunate. But that's been my experience with these conflicts. And they do turn out to be conflicts."

I asked a few more questions to end my interview with the biologist and thanked him for his time. Abby and I said goodbye to Tony, who was still talking to a group of folks who had attended the meeting. He looked more relaxed now than he had before the meeting had begun and even, I thought, appeared to be enjoying his new role as revolutionary environmental leader. He had proved to be good at it during his first meeting at the Opry Barn. Power to the people.

I reached for Abby's left hand and held it as we left the Opry Barn, walking into the parking lot to my car. It was dark now, and I could see a full moon rising in the direction of the river and lake. A slight breeze brushed across our faces and for a moment you could, if you tried, forget it was summer. I looked at Abby and then across the parking lot and saw the two sheriff's deputies were still there. We walked within ten feet of their patrol cars on the way to my car. One of the deputies smiled and waved. We waved back.

The drive home was purposely slow, and stars begin to fill the night as there were few electrical lights along the countryside. I drove at times with one hand on the steering wheel, and the other over Abby's shoulder tucked underneath her hair, where I could feel the back of her neck. We talked about the meeting and what might happen in the days and weeks ahead. She was excited with her part and the pictures she had taken at the Opry Barn. I played some music, but kept it low. She rubbed my arm and the back of my neck. I looked at her as much as I looked at the road. We talked some more about the river. Tonight's story would not appear in tomorrow's paper, Mickey had told me before we left. I could write a full story in the morning, and it would run the following day. No need to hurry.

It was around nine-thirty that evening when Tony finally left the Opry Barn, thanking the owners for allowing his group to use it free-of-charge and making plans to use it for other meetings. People were helping him. Their common love and appreciation for the river and lake was binding people together for this cause. People who voted differently, had different views on other issues, were united in support of their river and lake. Tony's authentic personality and leadership could hold them together for now.

It was a comforting thought for Tony as he walked toward his pickup truck to go home to his wife Rebecca and their two young boys, Jake and Adam. He was hoping that they were not asleep and he would have time to be with them and tell them a story about a heroic boy who saves his family from a monster that eats people. He tried to give them a hero story every night before he tucked them in. That was one of the things he loved doing. One of the many good things his father had done for him.

Maybe this thing that was happening to Tony and the folks who came to the Opry Barn tonight would end well, and the company would stop what it was doing to the river, Tony thought. But not without a fight. He got into his truck and pushed a ZZ Top tape into his eight-track player. He turned the volume up full. The two deputies who had been in the parking lot were gone before Tony left. They were the last to leave before Tony.

He would later recall that one of the last things he remembered was the beginning guitar licks from the ZZ Top song, "Lagrange," about a whorehouse in Texas. That was it. Those who got to him first had said he was unconscious for about three minutes. Death was close, they said. They could feel it.

He remembered something else before it all happened. Coming up fast behind him on Highway 300 was a car that he was certain belonged to Luther Wright, a Crisp County deputy. Not his patrol car, his personal car. Tony recognized the car through his rearview mirror because of its Confederate flag license plate and the extra set of headlights that he knew Luther used to illegally hunt deer at night. Tony had seen the car many times before that night at Stripling's Diner and the Gator Pit, and other places along the river and lake. That was the car that ran Tony off the highway that night at seventy miles an hour, and caused Tony to crash against a large pecan tree in the front yard of Jim Lassiter, one of the fishermen who had attended the meeting at the Opry Barn. Tony had guessed seventy, but it could've been faster.

"It all sounded like a bomb exploding. The way they did when I was in Vietnam," Jim Lassiter said. "For a moment I thought I was back in 'Nam. Damn, I was scared." It was Jim who had called the ambulance.

Tony didn't remember hearing anything. He didn't feel anything until hours later at the hospital. He never wore a seatbelt and hadn't on that drive home from the Opry Barn when he was slammed into the windshield, causing deep cuts on his face and head, and a concussion. When the paramedics removed him from his truck, still smoking and crumbled against a large pecan tree, Jim had taken a handkerchief from his pocket and wiped Tony's face, but the blood had not stopped. Jim had been waiting with his friend and fishing buddy when the ambulance arrived. Jim was thinking Tony could die in his arms like one of his buddies had in Vietnam.

"He ain't going to die, is he?" Jim said, to one of the paramedics as they put Tony on a stretcher and wheeled him toward the ambulance.

"I don't know, buddy," the paramedic said. "We'll do our best and then the doctors at the hospital will have him. He's in a mess right now. I just don't know how serious it is yet."

The two paramedics hurried away with Tony on the stretcher.

Tony moved his head slightly and moaned. It was the first sound that Jim had heard from him, but it wasn't much of one.

"You taking him to Crisp Regional?" Jim said.

"Crisp County Regional, that's right. We should be there in about five minutes," the paramedic said.

"Okay. I'll call his wife. I'll call Rebecca. I know her."

Jim turned away from Tony, his wrecked truck with smoke rising from the engine, the paramedics, and the ambulance and ran toward his house and to the telephone. As he dialed Rebecca Patrick's number, Jim could see out the kitchen window the smoke from the truck rising high in the night sky and the flashing red lights from the white ambulance speeding to Cordele. He saw a Crisp County Sheriff's Office patrol car and two men in uniform looking at Tony's truck. They had arrived moments before the ambulance.

# CHAPTER 10

Doctors took two hours to remove all the glass from Tony's face and head, and close deep wounds that required forty-seven stitches. He had a slight fracture in his right arm that they said should heal well in a few weeks, but required a cast. Tony was black and blue on his chest and neck from bouncing around in his truck like a pinball. He hurt in ways he had never hurt before. It would've been worse had he not been a rugged man and in good physical shape, the doctors said. He would have no permanent physical damage.

"You're just a lucky man," one of the doctors said. "It could've turned out different for you. It could've been awful." He was in his mid-thirties with thick dark hair and wearing his blue scrubs. He was looking down at Tony lying in a hospital bed five hours after the surgery ended.

"Thanks for what you did for me," Tony said.

He murmured his words because he had only been awake a few minutes and was still heavily sedated. He hurt everywhere.

Rebecca had arrived at the hospital fifteen minutes after the ambulance had the night before. She had found a neighbor to stay with Jake and Adam, and drove as fast as the ambulance that was carrying her husband. She would say later she didn't remember making the drive to the hospital.

"Who's with Jake and Adam?" Tony said.

He reached for his wife's hand.

She grasped it with her right hand and with her left, took a tissue from the nightstand next to Tony's bed and wiped tears from her eyes.

"Baby, they're fine. Delores from next door has them. You just need to rest. Everything's going to be all right. She'll take good care of them. She always does. The boys are fine. Don't worry about them."

"Of course, baby. Everything is going to be all right. Everybody's okay. Everybody's okay, everybody's okay."

His words grew weak and he stopped talking. A half minute later he was sleeping. He would need plenty of sleep and morphine for the next few days. Rebecca held tight to his hand and watched him as if he might try to get up and leave. She looked at him for ten minutes, her face grief stricken.

That morning at the *Albany Chronicle* the paper's police reporter for the outlying counties, Charlie Harrison, had picked up the story of Tony's wreck from a source in the Crisp County Sheriff's Office. Charlie walked over to my desk and told me what he had learned about Tony. I immediately called the hospital and was transferred to Tony's room. Rebecca answered.

"This is John Maynard with the *Albany Chronicle*. I want to find out how Tony Patrick is doing. Whom am I speaking with, please?"

"This is Rebecca, Tony's wife. And John we haven't met, but my husband has told me all about you and, of course, I've read your work. Tony's awful fond of you. Yes, he's going to be all right. He's going to be fine, thank God. It could've been worse. So much worse."

"How bad was he hurt?"

"His face and head are cut up pretty bad. And he has a fracture in his right arm. He's bruised black and blue, and has a minor concussion. He hit that big tree hard, and he could've easily been killed. Doctors say no permanent damage. God, he's lucky. Me and the boys are lucky. He's a good man, John."

"What can I do to help?"

"We're fine right now. I've got help at home. I know Tony will want to see you, but I'd wait a few days. He's going to be doing a lot of sleeping. The doctors say they want to keep him here for four or five days, maybe longer, so those wounds heal properly. So there's no problem. But he looks bad now. Real bad. He's in a lot of pain."

"I'll come up in a few days. Rebecca, how did this thing happen?"

"I don't know and right now I don't care. What matters is that my husband is alive. My children still have their father. I'll think about what caused it later. It just doesn't matter now."

"I understand, Rebecca. I'll see you in a few days. When he wakes up, tell him I called and asked about him. I think a lot of him and what he's doing for all the folks up there. What he's doing for the river."

"I will, John. I'll tell him you called. Thanks."

"Goodbye, Rebecca."

Tony and Rebecca had married when they were both twenty-two. She had taught second-graders in the Americus public schools for a few years, but when her first son was born she stopped teaching to stay home with him. She had not returned to the classroom. She was pretty, with light brown hair and striking blue eyes. In 1977 she had been crowned Miss Americus and came in third in the Miss Georgia Pageant. Tony didn't know her then, but had seen her picture in the paper and decided then that's who he wanted to marry. Tony had been in love with her since their first date at a Hank Williams Jr. concert at Georgia Southwestern College. She loved the music, and she loved Tony.

The *Chronicle* reported the accident in a five-paragraph story quoting a Crisp County sheriff's deputy and indicating Tony's leadership in the newly formed Save the Flint organization. The story said, before the accident occurred Tony had left the meeting at the Opry Barn and was on his way home to his family. The accident was "under investigation to determine the cause," and no charges had been filed. Tony had been hospitalized, but his injuries weren't "life-threatening." No one else was involved in the wreck, the story said.

I read the story three times before I put it away and thought about the things that Tony had been confronted with since we had taken our first boat ride together. Maybe this was just an accident. Tony was probably tired, and he could've fallen asleep on the way home. He wasn't intoxicated, I thought, knowing that Tony enjoyed a cold beer. There had not been enough time for him to drink himself drunk from when he left the meeting till he smashed into the pecan tree in Jim Lassiter's front yard. Tony occasionally liked a little marijuana buzz too, he once told me. It went well with ZZ Top.

What was the answer?

I picked up the telephone and called Abby, who was working upstairs developing pictures of debutantes. She had overlooked the story in the paper about Tony's accident. I told her about it and that Tony was recovering.

"John, what's happening to Tony up there? This isn't right. This may not be an *accident* at all. Somebody's out to get him, John. This is starting to scare me. This was no accident. I just don't believe it was."

"Abby. I'm not ready to even consider that. A dead snake, slashed tires, and getting beat up by two thugs, and this wreck. It's all coming fast, I agree but. . ."

"Well maybe this is just the next step, John. Maybe all that other stuff they did, whoever did those things, it didn't work and now they're trying something else. Something worse. It's a pattern. An awful pattern."

"I know you watch and love movies, but this story line I can't accept. I just can't believe someone was trying to kill him. That's what you're saying. Aren't you? Trying to kill him because he's gone public about the river. I can't buy it."

"I hope you're right, and it was just an accident. I don't want to be right about this."

"I don't want you to be, either."

We didn't speak for several seconds until Abby spoke again.

"Hello, Johnny Boy. Hello. Are you still there?"

"Yeah, yeah, I am, but I'm fading fast thinking about what you're saying. I'm having a hard time with all of this. Somebody has been after him. But to try to *kill* him on the highway? I don't know. I just don't know."

"I don't know either, John. But I'm thinking, I'm just thinking. What I'm thinking is making me sick to my stomach."

"I'm going to go see him tomorrow after work. I'll probably leave around four. Why don't you come with me."

"I will. I want to go with you."

"Okay. Count on it."

The next morning at work I helped a new young reporter re-write a press release from the governor's office about the state's economic outlook. The press release was only around seven hundred words, but the reporter was struggling with it. I had once needed that kind of help, too. It was hard for me to concentrate with my mind centered on Tony Patrick in that hospital bed all cut up and once so close to death. I thought about what Abby had said yesterday. I repeated this in my mind: *It was just accident. It was all just an accident.*

When Abby and I left the newsroom that afternoon, the August heat poured down on us like a bucket of burning metal. I had finally gotten the air conditioning fixed and other things had changed too. Not long into the drive, I pushed in an eight-track Bob Dylan tape, rested my hand on top of her left thigh, and we listened. We talked and listened some more. When Dylan sang, *You're gonna make me lonesome when you go. You're gonna make me lonesome when you go.* She leaned across the seat and kissed my right cheek. A few minutes later I pulled into the hospital parking lot in Cordele.

I parked, we got out and walked into the hospital holding hands. I talked to an elderly woman in a pink pinstripe dress behind the information desk. She was looking at names on a clipboard and next to her were two plants covered with white and red flowers.

"Good morning, Ma'am. We're here to see Tony Patrick. He was admitted two days ago. He's expecting us."

"Oh, yes, honey, I know Tony. He's such a good boy. I know his mommy and daddy. Great people. Tony helped my husband fix his boat a few years ago. My husband's dead now. Tony's going to be all right, don't you worry, honey. He's a tough, good boy. Room 307. He's in room 307."

"Thank you, Ma'am," I said.

We took the elevator to the third floor and walked past two men in wheelchairs waiting on nurses to take them back to their rooms. We saw Tony's room with the door slightly open. I knocked lightly.

"Hell, yeah we're home. But you can't come in unless you brought me some cold beer. Go away if you don't have beer. Beer with morphine, that's what I need."

"I don't have any beer, Tony. But I got Abby."

"Well, I'll be damned. She's a helluva lot better to look at then you, Mr. Reporter."

We walked into his room and toward his bed, where he was lying propped on three big, white pillows. Rebecca had left the room fifteen minutes earlier and gone home to take care of their boys. She was planning to return to Tony later that day. There were about a dozen bright green, yellow, and red flowered plants in Tony's room, sent from friends and family. Get well cards were lying on a table underneath a mirror. Baskets of fruit and candy were stacked in one corner of the room. But there was no beer.

There were no bandages on Tony's face and head, and the many dark black stitches looked perfect for a horror film. It would be a film that could cause nightmares. His face and neck were bruised black and blue, and he was, I thought, an ugly sight.

Scattered on Tony's bed were three fishing magazines, a book about America's polluted rivers, and a notebook he had been keeping the past few weeks with information about his efforts trying to stop the degradation of the Flint River. Tony hadn't been that thorough when he was a student at Georgia Southwestern College. Doctors had told him he needed to stay a couple more days in the hospital and soon after that they could remove the stitches. He was an impatient man.

"I was hoping me and Abby could get a boat ride today on *Cheap Sunglasses*. And then have a couple of cold beers with you at the Gator Pitt. Can we sneak you out of here? Are you ready?"

"I'd love to. But you need to talk to the nurse from hell. She just left a minute or so ago. She's the one with the butcher knife on her hip and a pistol in her pocket. That mean woman ain't goin' let me go nowhere. I'm stuck for a few more days. That's what the docs say, anyway. But what the hell do they know?"

Tony grinned and Abby reached for his left hand, squeezed for a moment and then let go.

"We wanted to come see about you," Abby said. "What can we do for you, Tony? How can we help you and your family?"

"Give me a beer, buy me a new truck, and help me and my family move to Alaska so I can get away from all this shit that's happen' to me. You and Mr. Reporter can handle that, can't you, Abby? That's what you can do for me. Right now I have a whipped ass."

"I was thinking more like bringing you something good to eat or babysitting your children," Abby said. "Helping Rebecca. Tell us what we can do."

"You've done enough by coming here. I'm goin' to be okay. I'm just ready to get out of this place."

"Okay, Tony," Abby said.

Tony began to talk about the details, the things he could remember about the wreck. Neither Abby nor I asked him to, but Tony began to speak about it anyway.

That night after Tony left the Opry Barn going north on Highway 300, a big car sped up directly behind him crashing into his back bumper. Tony cussed and hollered at whoever that driver was, he remembered. Tony went faster trying to elude the car behind him. He couldn't get away. That car kept coming and kept pushing. He struggled to keep his truck on the highway and, before he lost control of it, remembered seeing through his rearview mirror that the car pushing him had a Confederate license plate in the front and an extra set of headlights. His memory was clear about all of that, he said. When his memory served him again, he was waking up in the Crisp County Hospital after surgery.

"I got to tell you something about this. I haven't told Rebecca. I've told no one, but you need to near this."

"What is it? What are you talking about?" I said.

"That car that did this to me, I don't know who was driving, but that car belongs to Luther Wright. I promise you that was Luther's car. I swear it."

He said it as if Abby and I should know who he was talking about.

"Who's that? Who's Luther Wright?" I said.

"*Deputy Sheriff Luther Wright* with the Cordele Sheriff's Office. One of Sheriff Sonny Dupree's fine, upstanding, full-of-shit, lawmen. A prick. Total prick, John."

"Are you saying a cop ran you off the road? That a cop tried to kill you? Is that what you're saying, Tony?" I said.

"I don't know what I'm saying right now. But I do know that it was Luther's car ran me off the road. His personal car, not patrol car. I've seen him in the damn thing all over the place for years. Him and his fat partner riding around and drinking beer when they ain't on duty. Hell, maybe when they are on duty. I *know* that was his car."

I looked at Abby and then at Tony who had picked up one of his fishing magazines and began flipping pages, from front to back and then back to front. He didn't read a word. He didn't look at a picture. He kept flipping with his head down.

We sat down in two soft-cushioned tan chairs positioned on each side of Tony's bed. Both of us looked around the room as if there was something we were looking for but hadn't been able to find it. No one spoke for a few moments. Tony put down his fishing magazine and picked up another one. He flipped through it the same way he did the first one. I leaned back in my chair and stayed there for a few seconds then leaned forward.

"Now what? What are you going to do now?" I said.

"You're the one always on the front page. You tell me. You're the smart one aren't you?" Tony said.

"I wouldn't be on the front page without you."

"What are you going to do, Tony?" Abby said.

"When are you going to tell the sheriff's office what you just told us?"

"I'm not."

"What do you mean, you're not?" I said.

"Like I said, I'm not."

"You've got to tell them, Tony," Abby said.

"I told you, I'm not."

"You've got to tell the sheriff's office what happened that night," I said. "Tell them what you saw. Tony, this is crazy not to report this. Whoever did this to you needs to go to prison for a long, long time."

"Nope. Won't tell right now. Not now, anyway. And both of you better swear right now you won't tell anyone. You better swear it to me."

"Tony, think about what you're saying," Abby said. "You can't let somebody get away with running you off the road and trying to kill you. That's what they, whoever was driving, wanted to do. You have to report what you saw."

"I'm not going to the sheriff's office. I'm not calling the state patrol. And I'm not callin' the God-Almighty U. S. Army or the president of the United States. I got to wait and think about this thing for a few days. I got to figure out on my own the right thing to do."

"Tony, you were tired that night," I said. "It was dark. You sure that was Luther Wright's car? Do you know what you actually saw?"

"As sure as you love that pretty little girl in that chair over there." He nodded toward Abby.

"Maybe that car *belonged* to Deputy Wright, or maybe it was another car that looked like the deputy's," I said. "Maybe whoever it was, just came around you too fast and you lost control of your truck. I know you had to be tired after that meeting and from everything that's been happening to you. Maybe it was all just an accident."

"If it was, why didn't they stop and help?" Tony said.

"Good point, Tony," Abby said.

"Yeah, good point," I said.

"Maybe this, maybe that. *Feed a monkey and watch him shit!* Any man can believe anything he wants to believe. And so can a fool. Now John, my boy, I've been around you long enough to know you ain't no fool. I know what happened to me that night. I know what I saw. I don't remember much else, but I know the car that did this to me."

"Okay, okay, I wasn't there when it happened. Neither was Abby. Tony, what can I do? What do you want us to do?"

"Promise me you'll say nothing to no one. You got to swear it. This is big shit off the record. I mean don't even tell Rebecca. She's already a mess about all of this. Even before this, she'd wake up in the middle of the night crying and worried about what was coming next. Hell, I'm worried about her. I'm worried about my boys. I'll figure out what to do when I get out of this damn hospital. When I get strong again. I need some time to think."

"You got my word," I said. "I'll say nothing for now about this. I promise you that."

"Me too, Tony," Abby said. "I won't say anything to anybody. You got my word, too. I promise you."

Then the nurse from hell returned to Tony's room to check his blood pressure and other vital signs. Nothing else was said about the wreck. I watched the nurse work and thought of those deputies I had seen in Stripling's Diner weeks earlier. Was Luther Wright one of them?

# Chapter 11

A thunderstorm was crashing around us as we crossed the hospital parking lot toward my car. It had been clear and hot most of the time we were with Tony. Things changed abruptly. I ran holding Abby's hand while large raindrops pounded us both. The cool rain on our bodies felt good.

Water accumulated fast on the black asphalt and steam rose high. The water rushed into large concrete run-off pipes that would take it to the Flint River. Everything led to the river. Some things were natural and others weren't.

I drove out of Cordele and both of us looked for patrol cars from the sheriff's office. Neither one mentioned what the other was doing. We were thinking the same thing.

As we got closer to Lake Blackshear, the rain was heavier and making it hard for me to see clearly out of the windshield. Like my air conditioning had been, the windshield wipers were worn and needed replacing. I pulled into the parking lot at Stripling's Diner to wait out the weather. I parked close enough to the door to clearly read the painted white sign on the big window. *Stripling's Diner: Where Everyone's Family.* In the parking lot was a sheriff's patrol car with two men in uniforms sitting in the front seat. I turned my car off to wait.

"Do you think maybe Tony's wrong?" I said. "That he just *believes* someone in a car owned by a sheriff's deputy ran him off the road. Someone was trying to kill him. Sometimes people get things in their minds that aren't true, but they hold on to them for a long time. Maybe forever. But they're never true, and never will be true."

"Maybe so, John. But he sounded convincing to me. He doesn't seem like the kind of man to make up things."

"People who are wrong can be the most convincing sometimes. But they're still wrong."

"You're right. But something bad happened to Tony that night. And I just believe that he knows what he saw. I believe what he's telling us is true."

"You know how we can be sure?"

"No. Tell me. How?"

"When the rain stops, you can get out and go ask those two fellows in that patrol car what happened that night when Tony wrecked. Maybe Luther Wright is one of them."

I patted her left leg and looked into her eyes. Abby didn't answer but turned from me and looked out of the car window at the patrol car as the rain began easing, the thunder no longer heard. I started my car and drove away from Stripling's parking lot leaving the patrol car, and the men inside, behind.

In the distance, beyond the lake and toward Albany, we could see dark clouds still moving, low and fast, as fast as if they were late for something important that had already happened.

"Maybe I will ask them, John. Maybe I will. But not today."

"Yeah, you can do it later."

I took Abby home, and we had a couple glasses of chardonnay as the storm passed altogether. It was cooler now that the rain had come and gone. She cooked spaghetti, made green salad with red tomatoes, onions, and plenty of black olives. It was the way we both liked it. During the meal we talked about Tony and the river and nothing else. We slept naked under a ceiling fan that Abby said made her think of *Casablanca*, one of her all-time favorite movies. She quoted a few lines from Casablanca and each time she finished a sentence I kissed her lips. She had at least ten all-time favorite movies and an equal number of all-time favorite books. The fan cooled our bodies like the raindrops had done that afternoon in Cordele.

I left her house about seven the next morning and went to mine. I showered, changed clothes, and was in the newsroom a few minutes before eight. I told Mickey we had visited Tony in the hospital.

"Well, the son-of-a-bitch is going to live, right?" Mickey said.

"Right, Mickey. He's going to be okay."

"When's he getting out?"

"In a few days."

"Write a story about his accident and your hospital visit. He's a public figure now. And has been since your first story, Maynard. You helped make him one. Write the story."

"That's right. I will. I'll write what I know."

"Maynard, goddamnit, you need to call the sheriff's department up there, or the state patrol, whoever handled the damn thing, and find out the cause of the wreck. We don't need much, but we need a story and we need to run one tomorrow. If your man up there's going to continue to lead Save The Flint, the public needs to know. Don't you think?"

"Yes, you're right."

He lit the last Marlboro from a pack, crumbled the pack and threw it in the trash can next to his desk.

"I'll get right on it," I said, and walked away from Mickey's desk.

I wouldn't include everything I knew.

After Mickey's instructions, I called Tony at the hospital and got a few quotes I could use about his anticipated full recovery and that he planned to continue his leadership in Save The Flint. He said he was even working in the hospital, making phone calls to organize a board of directors and scheduling another meeting at the Opry Barn that would include environmental attorneys from Atlanta interested in offering their legal advice and support. Tony was still in this thing and determined in the same way he was when it had all started. I knew that before I made the call and got the quotes.

"I'll be out of here in a few days, and I'll return to the fight for our river and lake," Tony said. "We've got to keep putting the pressure on Transpower. We want our river and lake back the way they once were. I need a little more time to heal from the wreck."

He spoke slowly, giving me plenty of time to get the entire quote in my notepad.

The story would include what Tony said about planning further meetings and other ways, "maybe lawsuits," to fight what the company was doing.

"You ought not to be able to kill a river and get away with it," he said. "I don't care how many good jobs you provide for the community, or how much money you make for your shareholders. I plan to do what I can to stop it."

I got what I needed from Tony and then called Crisp County Sheriff Sonny Dupree.

"Sheriff, this is John Maynard with the *Albany Chronicle,* and I was hoping you'd give me some information about the wreck Tony Patrick was in the other night on Highway 300. I'm doing a follow-up story on the accident."

"Son, Tony who? What's your question again? I think we got ourselves a bad connection here. Where you calling from? China?"

"No, sir. Not China. Albany. Albany, Georgia."

I repeated the question. I thought the connection was fine.

"Oh, yeah, that feller was probably going too fast, but we haven't charged him with anything yet. We just don't know. But I know his family must be relieved that he's going to be fine. I know he's got a pretty wife and two young sons. That's a lot to live for. I know who he is."

"So the accident is still under investigation?"

"Yes, sir, it is. I'm going to send one of my deputies to visit with Mr. Patrick in a day or two. We don't want to get in the way of his recovery. Son, we here in this office have to respect that. Do you understand? We want to do what's best for people."

"Yes, sir, sheriff I understand. When will you conclude your investigation?"

"It won't be long, and we'll call you when we're finished. Or I'll tell you what, Mr. Maynard, you call us back in a few days and we'll have something for you. I promise you that. You call us anytime you want."

"Thank you, sheriff. I'll call again."

"Goodbye now, son,"

I wrote the story in about thirty minutes and gave the copy to Mickey. Dupree said he was going to send one of his deputies to speak with Tony. According to Tony that had already happened. That visit about killed him. If a deputy does show up at Tony's house,

Tony just might knock the hell out of him before anything is said.

The next day was Friday and Mickey had nothing scheduled for me that afternoon. I decided to drive back to the lake and talk to some other sources now that this movement against the company and for the river was underway and on the minds of many of our readers. Now it seemed that someone had tried to kill Tony, and I was almost ready to fully accept that idea. Tony, I believed, might be hard to kill.

I asked Abby to go with me that afternoon. Her schedule was free and she agreed and brought her camera, a notepad, and a book of poetry.

"John, do you know what John Adams once said?"

"John Adams? Doesn't he play shortstop for the Braves? Or is he a pitcher?"

"No, you must be thinking of Harry Adams or Adam Harrison. Or maybe not thinking at all."

"Well, uh, you mean President John Adams? President of the United States?"

"Yes, that's the one. You know what he said once?"

"The hell with the British! Let's fight, boys! Fight to the end!"

"No, smarty, he said, 'You're never alone with a poet in your pocket.'"

"That's just another reason why I love being with you. You talk to dead presidents."

"Not to them, about them."

"Who's in your pocket?"

"It's Arthur Rimbaud, the French poet. You know about him don't you?"

"No. You'll have to tell me all about him. Not Adams, the Arthur guy. Arthur who?"

"Oh I will, Johnny Boy, I will. It's Arthur Rimbaud, a French poet from the nineteenth century."

She pulled the book of Rimbaud's poetry from her purse. She had a page marked with a long bookmark full of quotes from her favorite novelists. She began to read from Rimbaud.

full of joy, with your mouth watering, rubbing your eyes. . .You went with tangled hair and shinning eyes, as on holiday mornings, little bare feet brushing the floor, to tap softly on your parents' door. . .You went in!. . .And then came the greetings. . .in your nightshirt, kisses, and fun all allowed!

When she finished, Abby closed the book and sat it on her lap. She looked at me and I at her, and I looked back again at the road.

"Don't you just love it, John? Isn't it the most beautiful thing you've ever heard? Tell me it is. Please tell me it is. Don't you love the way he used words? Oh, I wish I could do that. I so wish I could."

"I love it if you love it. One day, Abby. One day soon you'll use words the same way."

"I've read that a hundred times and it makes me think of all the fun I had with my mother and father. Of going into their room and bouncing on their bed with my pajamas on. Oh, the language is so beautiful. So beautiful, John. Don't you just love it?"

"I've never heard it, but I like it. Maybe I need to keep a poet in my pocket like you, Abby."

"I think you do, John."

"Okay, I will."

"You know I'm just an addict John, just an addict. I've been addicted to words since my mother read to me when I was a little girl. I'll never kick this addiction. I don't want to."

"I don't think you should."

We drove on talking about poetry and music and great novels and when we got to Lake Blackshear, I pulled into Stripling's Diner.

"Let's go in and order some sweet tea. No girl of the South should go without it. Even one who reads French poetry should drink it," I said.

"Oh, Johnny, those are the best kind of southern girls. Just like me. I like the Allman Brothers Band, too. And I do like sweet tea."

I stopped and parked the car, and she opened the car door and got out. We walked into the diner together. Flora, the waitress who I had met and talked with a few weeks before, was behind the counter serving a cheeseburger with onion rings to a man in dirty blue overalls. He covered the onion rings with ketchup. The food didn't stay long on his plate. There were about fifteen customers in the diner and most were farm workers eating their lunch.

We took a booth near where the deputies and the sheriff had been sitting the day I met Flora. A waitress came to our table and we ordered sweet tea, two salads with tomato and cucumber and Thousand Island dressing, and one order of onion rings. We split the onion rings. We ate and talked about what might happen next with the story, and if the river would ever be good again. Abby thanked me again for allowing her to cover the story with me. I was the lucky one, I thought.

Abby put the book of Rimbaud's poetry on top of the table, but she didn't open it. I had just finished my salad when I saw Willard Gentry, the storeowner from one of the back roads who I had interviewed during an earlier trip. He took a seat at the counter. "Hey, Mr. Willard. How you doin' today?" Flora said. "Sure is good to see ya." She brought him a tall glass of sweet tea with two pieces of cut lemon in it. He had not asked for it. Willard took off his straw hat, and sat on top of a stool at the white linoleum counter. He took a red bandana from his overalls' pocket and wiped the sweat off his face and from the top of his short-cropped, gray-haired head. He was hot. He put his hat back on.

"Hey, Miss Flora. You havin' a good day today?"

"Yes, sir. One of the best. Business is good. Life is the way it should be. Always is. No use complainin'."

"That's my girl. Always looking for the best. For yourself and everyone else."

"No other choice, Mr. Willard."

Willard took a drink of tea, didn't look at a menu and didn't order any food, but after Flora left him she returned a few minutes later with a grilled cheese sandwich, potato chips, and a sliced dill pickle. She sat the food in front of him.

"Thank you, Miss Flora."

"I hope you enjoy it."

"I always do."

Flora walked away from Willard to help other customers. After Willard's second bite from his grilled cheese sandwich, I got up from my table and told Abby I'd be right back. I wanted to speak with Willard Gentry. Abby stayed at the table and opened her book of poetry and began to read.

"Mr. Gentry, I'm John Maynard with the *Albany Chronicle*. We met a few weeks ago at your store. Remember?"

I extended my hand to shake Willard's.

"Son, I remember you. I saw the story you wrote. I've seen them all. Well, at least you quoted me right. You never know with reporters these days. You got it all about right. And I saw you at the Opry Barn that night. Pretty good work, son. So far."

He used a white a napkin to clean his right hand before offering it to me.

"I won't interrupt your lunch. I just wanted to say hello."

"You still looking for the end of the trotline, aren't you?"

"Still looking, and looks like I will be for a while. At least until the company cleans up the mess they've made. I don't think Tony Patrick is going to back down. It's a battle right now."

"I reckon you're right about that. They shouldn't. We shouldn't. There needs to be a battle."

"Seems to be the case."

"Well, son, your answers may not be where you're looking."

Willard took another bite from his sandwich, chewed as slow as the outside heat and then ate a potato chip. I sat down on the stool next to him. Willard took a long drink of sweet tea and wiped his face with the napkin that he had laid across his lap.

"We're just following the story wherever it takes us. Where do *you* think I need to look, Mr. Gentry?"

"Homer, son."

"Homer? Who's Homer? What's Homer?"

"You need to go talk to Homer. He's at the end of the trotline."

"Trotline?"

"Yes, sir. You heard me right."

"But I don't. . ."

Before I could finish Willard took over.

"Listen, son, I'm trying to help. And if you want to know more, you got to do more. You got to see Homer."

"What does he know?"

"He knows what he knows. You need to see him."

"You can't tell me any more than what you have?"

"I've told you who to see. That's enough."

"How do I find him?"

Willard told me Homer Jones was in his sixties and black and for most of his working life he had cut timber, mowed yards, worked on farms picking cotton, tobacco, watermelon, and anything else he could do with hands and arms and back to make money and feed his family. For the past ten years one of Homer's part-time jobs was as the yardman for the Crisp County courthouse. Willard told me where to find him.

Homer, Willard Gentry said, lived alone in a trailer at Camper's Haven, not far from the Gator Pit where I had put in the river for my boat rides with Tony, and where I had met Lard Ass, and where Tony had been beaten by two men before the wreck that almost killed him. I knew the way to Camper's Haven.

"Mr. Gentry, thanks for talking with me and thanks for the tip about Homer. I'm going to follow up this afternoon. I'll find Homer. I'll talk to him."

"It's your lead now, son. Be careful where it takes you."

"Yes, sir, we will."

I wondered about the "be careful" part.

Flora poured more tea into Willard Gentry's large plastic glass, and he began to eat the last few bites of his sandwich as I returned to my table where Abby was reading. I explained to Abby what he had told me.

"What does Homer know?" Abby said.

"I don't know what he knows. I tried to get more out of Gentry, but he didn't offer anything else. He just said go see Homer."

"What do you think Homer knows?"

"Good question. I don't have the answer to it, but I'm going to find out."

"Does he own a business that's been hurt by Transpower polluting the river? What does Homer do? What did that man tell you?"

"No, he cuts grass. He maintains the yard at the courthouse in

Cordele. Gentry said talk to him because you can't see for yourself what's on the end of a trotline."

"What does that mean? Other end of a trotline?"

"I'm not sure what it means. But, like I said, we're going to find Homer Jones and talk to him about the river. About our story."

"A grass cutter. Okay, John, let's go find this Homer fellow. A grass cutter on the end of a trotline. That's some lead Johnny Boy. I can't wait."

Abby closed her book of poetry and placed it back in her small brown leather purse. Her mother had bought the purse for her at a literary festival in Dahlonega, Georgia. Abby loved the new purse, and her notepad and a book of poetry fit perfectly. I paid the bill, and we headed to Camper's Haven. If nothing came of the lead, I thought, that's okay. I had Abby with me.

# Chapter 12

From a paved county road I turned onto Alligator Lane, a brown dirt road pocketed with holes on both sides and in the middle. More than ten miles an hour could damage a vehicle. Alligator Lane led to Camper's Haven where singlewide and doublewide trailers sat on about seventy-five acres of land along the backwaters of the Flint River. Life was slow here, like a pool of river water in a slough.

A thick canopy of water oak, live oak, cypress, and a few lone pines provided all-day shade for the trailers and those who lived in them. Spanish moss hung from most of the oak trees, and the still and quiet of that hot afternoon hung thick, too. I saw two mockingbirds chase a crow over one of the doublewides and Abby looked out the car window and saw the same.

"Mr. Crow is having a hard time, isn't he?" Abby said. "They sure are mean to him."

"Yeah, I think those mockingbirds work for Transpower."

"Why don't you put that in your story, Johnny Boy?"

"Maybe I will."

I realized I had forgotten to ask Willard Gentry exactly where Homer lived. I drove through Camper's Haven to the Gator Pit hoping to find Lard Ass there, and maybe he would know about Homer. I saw one truck in the parking lot, and assumed it was Lard's.

"I don't know where Homer lives. I forget to ask Mr. Gentry. We're going to stop at the Gator Pit and ask Lard Ass."

"Whatever you say, John. I'm with you, Johnny Boy."

"Come in with me. You need to meet Lard Ass. He's a real piece of work. You're going to love this guy. I want you to meet him since I've told you all about him."

"What's his real name? What did you tell me?"

"Lard Ass. That's his real name."

"John, I know that's not it. What is it?"

"Bubba Jackson. But that's not what they call him. I told you all about him. I quoted him in my first story. Remember? I even told you how he got his nickname."

"Okay, okay. I remember now. Let's go meet this Lard Ass. Maybe he can tell us where to find Homer."

I parked near the picnic table and big oak tree where Tony had gotten attacked. We walked over the hot asphalt parking lot to the store. I opened the door to Lard's, and we went inside. Lard was behind the cash register and saw us come in.

"Well, well, well. Here comes the man *himself*. Ain't you something, Mr. Big Shot Reporter."

"Maybe not the man himself, but I'm here again, Lard. Good to see you."

We walked to the cash register, and I shook hands with Lard.

"You got a pretty lady with you. Well, feed a monkey and watch him shit. Ain't you lucky, Mr. Reporter."

"Lard, this is Abby Sinclair. We've been working together on the stories up here. You may have seen her by-line on the pictures the *Chronicle* has run."

"Feed a monkey, honey! I've seen her name in the paper. She's right purty. Got all of her teeth it looks like to me. And no snuff in her mouth. Must not be from Alabama. This here's a high class woman, John. You don't deserve her."

Lard took off his weathered, lime-green John Deere cap with his right hand and bowed his head to Abby. He had a lot of dirty brown hair. Looked like it had been a week since he washed it.

"Lard, it's good to finally meet you. I've heard about you from John. He has told me a lot of good things about you and your store."

She extended her right hand to Lard. He took it and kissed the back of it.

"Well, your John may lie about a lot of things, Abby. But there *are* a lot of good things about me, I reckon. And the Gator Pit. Feed a monkey and watch him shit. I don't have time to list them all."

He spit tobacco juice in a gray metal spittoon sitting on top of his counter. His aim was exact.

"Now Lard, nothing but the truth and always the truth," I said.

"Always the truth, John, and one thing sure is true. Miss Abby here is the prettiest lady to ever been in these parts. I swear to it. Feed a monkey."

"Thank you, Lard," Abby said.

"No, thank you, Miss Abby."

Lard smiled and put his cap back on and Abby noticed tobacco stains on the white Atlanta Braves T-shirt that he was wearing. She smiled at him. He smiled back.

"Lard do you know a black man around here named Homer?" I said.

"That'd be Homer Jones. He's the only Homer I know 'round here."

"Mr. Willard Gentry didn't tell me where exactly he lived in Camper's Haven, but he told me I should talk to him about the river. Can you help us?"

"Feed a monkey, watch him shit, you damn right I can. Old man Willard and Homer go back a mighty long way. Back to the old days and old ways. That's what they say anyway. Homer lives back up Alligator Lane about eight or nine trailers on the right. He's got a fine tomato garden. You can't miss it. He gives me some tomatoes every year. Gave me some purty ones last week. He's got a couple of long-eared coon dogs that sleep all damn day. They wouldn't ass-scratch a flea. You can't miss them either."

"Does he work at the Crisp County Courthouse?" I said.

"Yes, sir. Sure does. Part-time. Got other part-time jobs too. A damn good man. Feed a monkey, Mr. Reporter. I'm telling you the truth. I've known Homer for years myself."

"We're going to try to see him today," I said. "Mr. Gentry said Homer may be able give us some help with the story. I'm not sure what he can tell us and Gentry didn't say exactly. He just said I needed to talk to him. He said Homer could help me."

"Old man Gentry has his ways, but I'd listen to what he tells you, Mr. Reporter man. He's been around here a long, long time and he knows."

"Knows what?" I said.

"Well, he knows a lot of things. Won't be a bad guy to talk to, Homer that is. If Gentry said it, you need to do it."

A car drove into the parking lot, and Lard looked out the window, unaccustomed to seeing much business since the river had gone bad. There were two men in the car. We looked through the front window of the Gator Pit and saw a brown late '70s Buick make two circles in the parking lot before leaving. It sped away and a dust cloud rose from the back of the car and faded into the cluster of cypress and oak trees shading the trailers on Alligator Lane. It left faster than it had arrived.

"That's all those two pricks do when they're off duty. They just ride around and drink beer. Hell, they may do that when they're on duty. Crisp County's finest, that's who they are. Feed a monkey and watch him shit. Sometimes that's all a man can do in this world. Feed the monkey and watch him shit. When you understand that, Mr. Reporter, well that's all you need to know about livin'. That's what my daddy used to say anyhow."

"Okay, I guess you're right Lard," I said. "I get it now. Feed the monkey and watch him shit. But who were the two guys that just pulled up in your parking lot and left?"

"Dupree's boys. They're sheriff's deputies. Like I said, Crisp County's finest."

"What's their names?" I said.

"Prick number one and prick number two. Or you can call them asshole number one and asshole number two. They'll answer to both of those."

"Sounds like they're well liked," Abby said. "Those are fine names, Lard. I bet their parents were proud of them with names like that."

"Yeah, they're well liked all right. About like having a snapping turtle attached to your ass."

"Lard, who were they?" I said. "They've got names. Even you have a *real* name."

"Feed a monkey and watch him shit, those are their names.

But sometimes they're called Clyde Ferrell and Luther Wright. Dupree has had them for, I guess, seven or eight years now. He hired them about the same time. They're just two poodles that Dupree has trained and keeps on a leash. Very well-trained monkeys."

Lard spit more tobacco juice, but missed the can and some landed on his counter. He cleaned it off with a piece of paper towel from a roll he kept on the counter.

"This here paper towel works real good," Lard said. "It's made by Transpower. Yeah, they'll kill a river, but they'll help you wipe up tobacco juice. Cleans it right up."

The car had come and left suddenly and I wasn't able to see the men inside. I didn't know if they were the same two deputies I had seen eating with Sheriff Dupree at Stripling's Diner. I was certain of the name Luther Wright.

Tony was certain from his hospital bed that it was Luther's car, with its Confederate flag and an extra set of high-powered headlights for deer shining, that had run him off the road after the Opry Barn meeting. Someone had intended to kill Tony that night. That's what Tony believed, and now I was coming around to the same way of thinking. Standing with Abby and Lard inside the Gator Pit that afternoon, I thought about how certain Tony was that it had been Luther's car. Since I started covering the river story, I had regularly seen patrol cars on the highways and dirt county roads and parking lots. I thought then they were keeping the county safe. Now I wasn't sure about that.

"Why you think they drove in and out of here?" I said. "What're they up to?"

"Hell, man, like I said, that's what they do. They ride 'round and drink. At least they didn't leave any empties in my parkin' lot this time. They don't bother anybody, they just ride and drink. They're up to whatever Dupree tells 'im to."

"That's not what you'd expect from the police," Abby said. "That's not a good example for the public."

"I guess not," I said.

"I reckon you're right, Miss Abby, but they don't care nothing about a good example," Lard said. "Things can be different up here on the river. Feed a monkey."

We walked away from the window and said goodbye to Lard. The car and the deputies inside of it were long out of sight. We followed Lard's directions and drove back up Alligator Lane where the Buick had disappeared. I stopped my car at the ninth trailer on the right where several red tomatoes were hanging from plants supported by silver wire cages. They were ripe tomatoes that needed picking soon. Four-foot-tall wire fencing encircled and protected the plants. The hound dogs weren't a threat to the plants. They were sleeping under the steps that led to the front door of the clean, white trailer. We parked and got out of my car, but I was hesitant about approaching big dogs I didn't know. Both of them woke up and saw Abby and me walking toward the trailer, then returned to their naps. Just like Lard said.

A brown 1969 Chevy pickup, looking freshly washed, was parked in the driveway next to a fifteen-foot-long johnboat with a trolling motor. Inside the boat were three cane poles strung with lines, hooks, sinkers, and bright orange bobbers. The poles were next to an empty cricket bucket and a white ice chest. Standard equipment at Camper's Haven. We walked toward the trailer.

Abby was next to me, but stopped when she saw the tomato plants up close.

"John, I just want to take a look at these tomatoes. They remind me of the ones my mother grew when I was a girl. Mom could grow some big, delicious tomatoes. Still does. I loved them, my dad loved them, we all loved them. You need to try them sometime, Johnny Boy. I'll just be a minute. I'll be right there."

"Okay, I'm just going to knock and see if he's home. He looks to be. I'm assuming that's his truck. A nice truck, too. You have fun looking at those tomatoes."

Abby walked to the tomato plants that were partly shaded from the mid-afternoon sun. They received enough sunlight for full growth. She stood over them as I knocked on Homer Jones' door. The dogs didn't move.

Five seconds after my knock, Homer opened the door. He was about six feet tall and one hundred and seventy-five pounds,

I guessed, lean and with the look of an athlete. Still an athlete, I thought. He had a white T-shirt on, jeans, and his modest Afro had a few specks of gray. He looked fit.

"I'm John Maynard with the *Albany Chronicle*. Are you Homer Jones?"

"Yes, sir. That's me."

"Can I talk to you just for a few minutes? I've got a question or two about the story I've been working on involving Transpower and what's been happening to your river up here. It looks like you're a fisherman, too."

I turned to look at the johnboat in Homer's front yard.

Homer stood in the doorway and cold air from his window air conditioning unit, humming hard, hit me in the face. It felt good and I wanted to be hit again.

"What about, sir? Why me? Why you want to talk with me?"

"I talked to Willard Gentry today and he suggested I come speak with you about this story I've been covering. I know it's important to everybody up here, and I'm just trying to learn as much as I can. So I followed Mr. Gentry's advice. That's why I'm here. Mr. Gentry sent me here."

"Mr. Maynard, I don't reckon I'd be much help to you and your newspaper. Everything that needs to be said has been said, best I can see. I bin readin' your stories."

He rubbed his chin with his right hand and looked at me and then seemed to be looking beyond my car into the dusty road, heat, and trees. All the way to the river. He looked in a way, I thought, that indicated Homer himself did not believe what he just said. He appeared to be looking for someone else to arrive at his trailer. I waited a few seconds before I replied.

"I just got a few questions. I won't take much of your time. If you don't want me to quote you, I won't. I understand if you don't want your name in the paper. Mr. Gentry said you could help me."

Homer Jones hesitated again, and I waited.

"Well, sir, I don't have much to say but I reckon it won't hurt nothin' if you come in and talk for a while. It's so hot out there the frogs have lost their minds and think they're crickets. Crickets think they're birds. Heat can make people crazy, too, if they ain't careful. Yes, sir, if they ain't careful, people go crazy too. It happens all the time."

I walked into the trailer and Homer closed the door behind us. Homer told me he lived alone after his wife Melva died last year from breast cancer three days before their wedding anniversary. When she died, Homer and their two children were there in the trailer with her, where she wanted it all to end. Had she lived three more days, she would've celebrated her and Homer's forty-fifth wedding anniversary. She fought hard to go three more days, but just couldn't, Homer said.

"God took her. She's okay now. No more sufferin' for my Melva."

Because of his hard work and the money she earned cleaning homes for the wealthy, Homer and Melva saved enough to send both their children to Albany State College, where they earned their degrees. Both had become teachers and moved to Atlanta. They had done well. Melva and Homer years ago set out to be certain of that.

In the trailer there were pictures of President John F. Kennedy and one of Robert, his brother. They were in black and white and both men were smiling over Homer's television set. On the other side of the den was a picture of civil rights leader Dr. Martin Luther King, Jr., taken in the early 1960s when he was arrested while marching in Albany.

There was a green-flowered sofa and two identical tan vinyl recliners that Homer had bought for him and Melva a week after she was diagnosed with cancer. He was hoping that they would help her. They did, but it wasn't enough. His home was clean and orderly, I thought, as I looked at the pictures along the walls. There were several of Melva and Homer's two children. Big smiles everywhere.

"I bet you'd like some lemonade, wouldn't you?" Homer said.

"Yes, sir, Mr. Jones, that does sound good. I'll take a glass."

Homer walked into the kitchen and took two tall plastic glasses with yellow flower designs from the cabinet. He opened the freezer to his refrigerator and used a large metal spoon to scoop ice into the glasses. On the counter was a white plastic two-quart container of lemonade made from frozen concentrate, but Homer had cut up a

# DEAD RIVER

whole lemon and squeezed all its juice into the container. Homer filled both glasses with lemonade and returned to the den where I was still standing and looking at pictures on the walls.

"Here you go, Mr. Maynard. This here's the best drink around." Homer handed a glass to me.

"Please, just call me John."

"Yes, sir, yes, sir, I will. You just call me Homer. That'll do fine. Just fine."

Then I thought about Abby being outside in the heat.

"Homer, my partner Abby, she works with me at the paper, is outside admiring your tomato plants. She's my photographer. I bet she's hot by now, and I need to go see about her before we get started."

"Well, go out and get her and get her out of the heat. Bring her in where it's cool, and I'll pour her some lemonade. That heat's a killer today. Has bin every day."

"She said your tomatoes were the best she'd seen in a long time, and they reminded her of the ones her mother grew when she was a girl. She still grows them."

"Go get her now, John. She don't need to be out there any longer in that heat. It's hot enough to make a snake stand up and walk to church and pray for rain."

I walked out of the trailer and over the two sleeping hound dogs, and past Homer's johnboat, and then to his tomato plants where I had left Abby a few minutes earlier. I didn't see her. I saw nothing but the tomato plants. I then walked around the back of the trailer thinking maybe Abby had found something back there, a peach tree, a grapevine or something that reminded her of her mother's love for things of the earth. Back there, Homer had a smooth cement patio with black iron lawn chairs circled around a grill and a large umbrella. I still didn't see her there.

"Abby! Abby!" I called out loud enough for the next four trailers to hear me.

I walked around the trailer and then back to the tomatoes again. I looked all the way down Alligator Lane, and saw dust behind a car about to leave Camper's Haven. Dust was flying high. The car was going fast, too fast for the dirt road it was on.

"Abby! Abby!"

Now hollering it loud enough that if Lard was in the Gator Pit's parking lot he would've heard me. I kept calling her name. I heard nothing in return.

I looked around Homer's trailer again and to as many trailers as I could see, as if looking harder would make her appear. Then I recognized something lying on the ground next to the tomato plants. It was Abby's small leather purse her mother had given her. Next to her purse was the book of Rimbaud's poetry, and next to that her reporter's notepad and pen. I picked up her purse, book of poetry, notepad and pen. I returned to Homer's trailer and went inside.

"She's gone. She's gone, Homer. Her purse and book are in your yard, but she's not there. I don't know what's happening. I left her by your tomato plants and now she's gone."

"What you mean she's gone? Gone where?"

"Just gone. I left her looking at your tomato plants, like I said, and now I can't find her. Her name is Abby Sinclair. She's gone."

"Let's step out here and see a bit. Maybe she went to another trailer to talk about somethin'. Maybe she saw a friend. Someone she knows. I spect that's what happened here."

"I hope so. I just hope you're right."

We walked outside the trailer and stood next to Homer's johnboat, and both of us looked toward the trailers nearby and up and down Alligator Lane. We saw no cars or trucks on the dirt road full of holes. It was quiet. No dust was flying. I kept looking into the distance as if Abby would emerge from one of the trailers, slide down a tree trunk, or fall gently from the sky and land on her feet next to me. The joke would soon be over and we would have a good laugh, a real good laugh. She probably saw someone she knew, like Homer said.

"Did you say you talked to Lard before you found my place?"

"Yeah, that's right. Lard told us about you. Where you lived."

"That's where she is then. She went back to the old Gator Pit for somethin'. Maybe to tell Lard somethin' or buy somethin' to drink."

"I'll find out."

I left Homer and got into my car and drove the quarter of a mile or so back to the Gator Pit. I parked next to the front door and got out and ran inside.

"Where's Abby? She's here isn't she? Where is she, Lard?"

Lard was watching a *Mayberry* rerun on television and was laughing at a scene where Barney, the deputy sheriff, had arrested the town drunk, Otis. The television was loud, and so was Lard's laughing. He didn't hear me come in and ask about Abby.

*"Lard, where's Abby!"*

Lard turned away from his television set behind the counter and stood up from the torn black wicker chair he had been sitting on. He had heard me the second time.

"Abby? Feed a monkey and watch him shit, son, she left with you. Are you losing your mind up here in this heat?"

"I think I am. I can't find Abby."

"What do you mean you can't find Abby? I just saw her a few minutes ago with you. How do you lose someone that purty?"

"Have you seen her since we left?"

"No, hell no. Hell, I ain't seen anybody since you left except Barney and Otis. And Otis is in damn jail. Feed a monkey, watch him shit. He likes jail. Did you find Homer?"

I looked around the Gator Pit the same way I had outside of Homer's trailer when I was looking for her. It was only me and Lard and Barney and Otis.

"Yeah, I found Homer, but now I can't find Abby. She's gone."

# CHAPTER 13

Abby had taken her notepad and pen from her purse, and had begun writing as she stood outside the trailer, while inside Homer was pouring lemonade for me. She stood over the tomato plants and wrote:

> *I saw her hands dig into the earth when*
> *I awoke early spring mornings*
> *Before the birds were singing*
> *She had her gloves on moving*
> *From plant to plant to plant*
> *   Moving, moving, moving*
> *Shoveling, pushing, pulling, digging*
> *Carefully, carefully, carefully the*
> *The same gentle way she bathed me*
> *And my brother and sister when we*
> *Were babies…*

Then the pen had fallen out of her hand onto the ground where I found it. Her arms felt like an electric shock had been sent through them. It was a feeling she had nothing to compare to. Whoever had her, there was no getting away from him. Struggling was useless. Someone put a black hood over her head one second after her arms had been snatched, and tied behind her back with a black electrical cord. The knot was pulled tight and pain shot through her wrists. She was about to scream. Then she felt two hands cover her mouth with thick tape. She did scream. No one heard anything.

Then someone picked her up and when that happened she kicked her purse that she had laid on the ground before she had begun writing about her mother. Her book of poems tumbled out of her purse onto the ground. Now she was across someone's shoulders being carried like a duffel bag. She was carried several feet and put into the backseat of a car. The engine was running and two people got into the front seat. She could see nothing and had to breathe through her nose with the tape tight around her mouth. The car pulled away from Homer's trailer and dust flew up behind it.

Nothing had been said. Thirty seconds after they grabbed her, the car she was in sped out of Camper's Haven. They were gone.

Five minutes passed from the moment she had been taken before either one of the men said or did anything other than drive the big brown Buick with the Confederate license plate from Alligator Lane onto a series of dirt roads taking them deeper into the thick swampland along the east bank of the Flint River, now about fifteen miles north of Lake Blackshear. Then someone jerked the tape from Abby's mouth. It hurt her. Abby's whole body heaved. She was frightened like no other time in her life. Were they killers?

She could breathe easier now, but she still couldn't see. They had left the hood over her head. The car's air conditioning was flowing full, but she could feel her face beginning to sweat as drops began to roll off her forehead and cheeks and onto her beige sleeveless blouse. She was too scared to talk and would not do so. Her hands were tied, but were trembling as if she were an old woman with a debilitating illness. She whispered to her hands to stop, but they did not. *"Stop it. Please stop it."* They couldn't. She spoke to them as a patient mother would trying to convince a child to behave.

The car had slowed to around thirty miles an hour now, after almost doubling that speed after they had taken her from Homer's trailer, put the hood over her, tied her arms, taped her mouth, and driven away. In spite of her fear, she could feel that the vehicle she was in had slowed.

Clyde Ferrell was driving and his partner, Luther Wright, had reminded him to slow down after they had left Alligator Lane.

"Go slow so folks won't know any different," Luther said. "We don't want to be seen with her, now do we Clyde? Take it slow. Take it real slow. We're safe now."

Luther knew he had to repeat things many times to Clyde in

the same way a first-grade teacher might talk to her class. It upset Clyde when Luther talked that way to him. Luther didn't care about his feelings, never had. It had been like that since they both became deputies years earlier.

"Dad-gum-it! No, I mean goddamnit, Luther don't, please, *please*, don't tell me what to do all the time. I'm tired of it. You mean to me all the time. Well, most of the time anyway. I know what I got to do. We sure been over it enough, ain't we?"

"Somebody's got to tell you what to do, and I'm that somebody. I best tell you or you won't do right. Clydey, I ain't mean to you, I just want this thing to go right. Now we done talked about all this before. We been over and over and over it."

They had both pulled off their black hoods, but left Abby's on her head. She could see nothing but blackness.

They were big men, in their mid-thirties, both around two hundred fifty pounds and almost identical in height at about five ten. Without their faces, their bodies could be twins. Luther had an Army tattoo on his left forearm from his time in the Vietnam War. The tattoo said, "To fight and die for your country!" He had a scar over his left eye about two inches long, but it hadn't come from a North Vietnamese communist. He got drunk one night in Saigon and challenged a fellow soldier to a knife fight. The soldier he fought needed fifteen stitches. Luther had been plenty drunk, but he was still quick, and meaner than the other soldier. When Luther squinted his scar from the knife fight became more visible, and he did so whenever he looked directly at something. Did it every time. Didn't matter what it was, and how far away he was from it.

Now Clyde wondered if Luther had gone too far as he looked in his rear view mirror and saw Abby hooded, hands tied, and trapped in the backseat. Since they had became deputies, if Sheriff Dupree didn't tell Clyde what to do, Luther did. Clyde complained about it sometimes, and called Luther a "mean, mean man," but not to his face. In the end he would do whatever Luther said. It had been that way since they started working together.

Clyde had dropped out of high school after two years in the

ninth grade. His father had sold moonshine and, later, marijuana. Legal work he rarely had. He had been in prison once for armed robbery. Clyde's father more than once said his boy had "a slow case, a mighty slow case, of the slows." His father had dropped out of school himself and could barely read and write. Clyde was ten when his father was shot and killed by an outraged customer complaining of weak moonshine. The customer was drunk at the time. Clyde's mother, two months later, left Georgia for California without Clyde and her two other children. For the next few years Clyde was in and out of foster homes, and was taking care of himself by the time he was fifteen. Mostly living on the street. Clyde sold moonshine once, had worked in the pulpwood business and the watermelon fields. Never worked at one place very long until he became a sheriff's deputy.

"How in the hell did he end up a deputy?" folks who knew him said. "The boy can hardly read and write."

Clyde didn't squint his eyes like Luther. He looked hard and wide-eyed at everything he saw, no matter how far away or how close it was. Whatever he was looking at seemed to confuse him. Luther played "Big Boss Man" to him, as Clyde said, giving orders regularly, even telling him when he could take a piss and when he couldn't. Luther told Clyde what to do in a degrading way, as a prison guard might speak to an inmate. It was easier for Clyde to take orders than to think on his own. Clyde knew it was true, and it always had been that way for him. He knew that much about himself, but he'd never say it. It bothered him to think it.

When Luther told him that he'd be the one to grab "the bitch girl from the newspaper," then drive the car out of Camper's Haven and later do what had to be done to her, Clyde looked away from him and bit his lower lip and said nothing. He would do it all right. He didn't like it, but he would do it anyway. He had done these kinds of things before, always following the instructions of others.

Clyde kept his black hair cut so tight it was difficult to tell what color it was. He had massive shoulders and arms without ever lifting any weights other than the twelve and sometimes sixteen-ounce beers. His head was big and most people who saw him for the first time would stare a moment or two at it. In grade school, the mean boys and girls teased him by calling him "planet head." It was big enough to be a small planet, they said. Clyde still remembered what they said. It still hurt him all these years later.

"Oh, no, here comes planet head, he's going to crash into the earth! Look out! Look out everyone! We're all goin' die!"

When he was in the seventh grade another boy, bigger than Clyde, teased him about the size of his head one day during recess. Clyde took it for a while, asked the boy to stop over and over, but he didn't. Then Clyde could take it no more. Clyde's face turned red like a traffic light, and he hit the tormentor with his right fist so hard that the boy was hospitalized and needed surgery to correct the damage. Clyde had always been a lot stronger than most boys, especially when he got angry. Now he was stronger than most men.

Luther had to remind Clyde, with Abby in the backseat, to slow down and not draw attention from anyone as they were headed for a cabin deep in the woods.

"I'll do right Luther and you ain't got to say it but one time and one time only. I don't like it when you tell me what to do over and over and over and over again. I promise I'll do right, Luther. I just don't like it when you say the same thing over and over and over."

"Holy Jesus, Clydey, I'm just tryin' to do what's best for me and you. I don't mean nothin' by it. I wish you'd just be quiet and quit your bitchin' 'cause it won't help anything. You should know that by now. Everything is goin' be good. I promise you."

"Don't call me Clydey. I don't like it because you treatin' me like a little boy again. I don't like it, and I done told you that a million times. I don't like it when you treat me like a little boy."

"Okay, okay, Clydey – I mean Clyde. I'm sorry."

"You best be sorry. I'm Clyde not *Clydey*. Always Clyde."

They passed Willard Gentry's store where a few trucks were parked, but no one was outside on the chairs and benches. They continued for another mile or so and turned off a paved road and onto a dirt road lined with oak, pine and thick green underbrush. They passed no other vehicles.

# DEAD RIVER

Luther Wright opened the metal glove compartment and took out an unopened pack of Red Man tobacco that was sitting on top of a thirty-eight caliber pistol. The gun was not in a holster. He opened the tobacco and got a wad in his right hand and pressed it into the shape of an egg. He placed the wad in the right side of his mouth. He closed the package of Red Man, and placed it on top of the pistol. Then he closed the glove compartment, banging it and startling Abby. She twitched in the backseat, not knowing what was coming next.

"Can I have some, please, Luther? Please can I have some, too?"

"Sure, Clyde, I'll give you all you want when we get her inside. Just wait to when we get her inside, then you can have all you want. I promise. You're doin' good."

"Thanks, Luther. That makes me feel better. I like it better when you're that way to me. I like your Red Man. It tastes the best. Better than anybody's."

Clyde was now driving on a red dirt road lined with two gullies about three feet deep where the water rushed after heavy rains on the way to the Flint River. Neither man spoke for the next couple of minutes. Abby's hands had stopped shaking. Her heartbeat wasn't normal, but nothing else was either. She was going to try to talk and didn't know if she could.

"Where are you taking me? Who are you? Where you taking me? Why are you doing this to me?"

"Oh, purty baby, we're goin' to have a fun time," Luther said. "A lot of fun together tonight. Don't you worry one little bit. Me and my good buddy here are goin' to take good care of you."

He turned around to look at her when he spoke and she could smell the beer, tobacco, and putrid body odor. The last time she had smelled something that bad, she was on the boat ride down the Flint River.

Luther used his left hand to pat her right knee much the way a man does to a good dog. She jerked her leg away from him.

"Stop this car and let me go! I promise I won't tell anybody about this. Just stop and let me go, *please!* Stop the car and let me go."

"I like it when a purty girl says *please!* Don't you, Clyde? It makes me feel good all inside."

"Yes, sir, Luther. I like it real good. Just like you. Just like you, Luther."

Clyde had both hands on the steering wheel and was looking into the rearview mirror at Abby.

"Well, now, honey we ain't goin' do that because we all come this far together and got a ways to go. You just relax and enjoy this nice cool ride. My buddy here is the best damn driver in this county and, anyway, it'd be too hot for you to walk back where we got you from. We just couldn't allow that. We're goin' be good to you. I promise you that."

"What do you want from me? I've never done anything to you. I don't even know who you are. Where are you taking me?"

"We'll take care of all that later," Luther said. "Don't you worry now. Just relax, honey."

"That's right purty baby. Like Luther said, you just need to relax."

The big brown Buick turned onto the final dirt road and drove by a green street sign leaning almost parallel to the ground that read End of The Line. For five miles the car went slow, passing thick woods that occasionally gave way to large cotton and peanut fields. They crossed a railroad track that hadn't been used since the 1950s. A white-tailed rabbit sat on the right side of the road, and didn't move as the Buick eased by. The animal looked the other way. A half mile past the rabbit, the road led to an A-frame log cabin with a shiny metal roof. At the cabin, the road stopped.

Behind the cabin was a white tattered singlewide trailer in need of repairs. That's where Clyde lived. He lived behind Luther. Beyond the cabin and the trailer, the land was covered in tall pines and scattered live oak trees with long sweeping saw grass underneath. The river was a half a mile away through the woods. It was the end of the line. Clyde turned the Buick into the gravel driveway near the front porch of the cabin and Abby heard the tires cut and grind in a clear and distinct way, as if she had been concentrating on a line from a Rimbaud poem. The car had stopped. Her senses were alert now. She didn't move. Her hands shook again, but not as bad as the first time. She could feel her heart beat. She was sweating more now.

"Okay, purty little baby, we've come home now and me and you and Clyde are all goin' to have lots of fun tonight. And you goin' to like it, I promise you that. Later the Big Man may come see you. Won't that be *special*, if the Big Man comes out."

"Oh, boy, I hope he does! He needs to see we done good again. We done good, ain't we Luther? Maybe he'll give us our money when he comes. We deserve it now, don't we Luther?"

"Yeah, Clyde we done good again. He might be a bit surprised to see our new purty baby. I bet he's goin' to be right proud of us. I'd like to see that money too, Clyde."

"Where am I? I want to know where I am. *Please take this hood off me!* I want to know where I am."

"Oh, no, sister baby if I up and do that somethin' bad might happen," Luther said. "That won't be good for you or me. Like I said, you just need to relax. Everything is goin' to be all right."

Her voice had grown weak again. Shaking even more now. It took all of what she had inside of her just to speak.

"I'm begging you, just untie my hands and let me take my hood off, and I'll walk away from here. I won't look at anything or anyone. I promise. I'll walk away and never tell anyone about this. I promise you, Luther. Clyde, will you please help me?"

Her wrists hurt badly since she was taken. Her hands continued to tremble.

"Sweetie pie, my little sweetie pie, you're here now with me and Clyde and it's all goin' to be all right. It's goin' to be good."

Luther reached around a second time facing Abby and slapped her across the face. Now her face hurt worse than her wrists and arms. She didn't make a sound. She was still alive, she thought.

"Luther, you told me there ain't goin' be none of that. Now why did you go and do that to her? She was being good. She was being real good."

"You just do what I say, Clyde. Don't worry about nothin' else but what I say. I'll take care of everything. Now you get the girl and bring her in just like we planned. Do it now, Clyde. Just like we planned."

Luther got out of the car and walked up the front wooden steps, painted fresh green, and walked into the cabin. There was a screen door, and then a wooden one. Both were unlocked. Clyde got out of the front seat and opened the back door on the driver's seat and reached in and grabbed Abby's left arm and pulled her out of the car. He wasn't rough like he had been at Homer's garden where she was taken. He was easy with her.

"Watch your head, Little Missy. I don't want you to get hurt."

Clyde got her out of the car, and Abby stood on her own. Her legs shook and her right one collapsed, and she hit the gravel with her knee. Clyde helped her up without hurting her. Again he was not rough with her. He had both his hands on each of her arms from behind her back. When she was standing on her own, he told her to keep walking. She followed instructions. He stopped her at the steps that led inside the cabin.

"Now, I ain't meanin' to hurt you any. You goin' have to step up just three times before I get you in Luther's cabin. You'll like it better in there. Luther's got a nice cabin. Real nice."

"I don't want to be in there, Clyde. Please *help me!* Don't hurt me. Don't take me in the cabin. Please don't."

"Just keep walkin' Missy. Everything's goin' to be all right. Just like Luther said."

She walked up the steps and was standing on the porch made with long pieces of heart pine that had been recently coated with a red varnish. Luther had done some of the work, but Clyde had done most of it. Clyde opened the screen door. Luther had not closed the wooden door that was covered with the same varnish. Clyde placed his right hand in the middle of Abby's back and guided her into the room. Just as if they were a couple attending a debutante dance.

Luther had placed a gray wrought-iron chair in the middle of the den where there was a large stone fireplace with an eight-point deer head above it. On both sides of the head were two ten-pound large-mouth bass that had been mounted. There was a white wicker sofa in the den and a black vinyl recliner. It was a clean, well-kept cabin. The chair in the middle of the room was for Abby.

When Clyde brought Abby in, Luther had pulled a beer from the refrigerator next to the black kitchen stove. He opened it, and took a long drink. Stopped and took another long drink.

"Put Miss Purty right there in that ole chair," Luther said. "Keep her hands tied for now. This chair is just for her. She'll be comfortable here. Won't you Miss Purty?"

With his finger he tapped the top of the kitchen counter as if he was preparing for a long drum solo. He took another drink of beer.

Clyde walked Abby to the chair in the center of the room. She felt the cool air in the cabin from Luther's single window unit. She was drenched in sweat, and could feel it dripping off the end of her nose.

"Sit straight down now and rest," Clyde said. "You goin' to be fine here with us. I won't let anything happen to you that's bad. I promise you that. It's all goin' to be okay. Isn't it Luther?"

Luther didn't answer.

Abby sat down and her tied hands kept her back straight as if she had won first place in a posture contest. She was still hurting. Wrists, arms, and face.

Luther walked from the kitchen to where Clyde and Abby were and stood looking over her with his beer in his right hand. With his left hand he rubbed her left leg from her knee to her thigh.

"*Get your hands off me!*"

She kicked hard at Luther with her left leg. She missed.

He slapped her harder than he had when they were in the car. She moaned and stopped kicking.

"You ain't goin' do that to me Miss Purty bitch. We'll have lots of fun later. You need to relax and enjoy it. Just like I said. I'll make you relax if I have to."

"Don't touch me! Don't ever touch me again!"

"Well, well, I reckon I like a little fire in my women. Don't you Clyde? Don't you like a little fire in your women? Oh, I forgot, you're scared of women aren't you Clydey?"

"I said don't call me Clydey. Remember. And I done told you a million times, I ain't scared of women, I'm just too busy for a girlfriend. Luther, we don't need to do those things to her, do we? I don't think you should, Luther. Let's don't be that way to her. That's not what you said was goin' happen at your cabin. This ain't right."

"It's right if I do it, Clyde. And don't ever, *ever* again tell me what to do. You understand?"

"I understand."

He squinted at Clyde six inches from his face. Clyde turned away from Luther and looked at one of the mounted largemouth bass on the wall. His mind was confused. Then he looked at the floor near where Abby's feet were resting. He kept his head down for thirty seconds. Then he raised it up to speak.

"I'm sorry. I won't ever again. I'll do what you say Luther, and it'll all be all right. Won't it? I'll do what you say. Won't it all be all right?"

"That's better, Clydey, I mean Clyde. Of course it will. Just like I told you. Everything's goin' to be okay."

Clyde walked away from Abby and sat down in the wicker sofa and looked at her as if she represented something he could not explain. Luther sat down on the other side of the sofa away from Clyde. He had taken the last drink from the beer, and tossed his empty toward a large gray metal trashcan on the other side of the room. He missed the trashcan, and the empty beer can hit the floor. Then Luther looked at Abby, knowing exactly what she represented.

Abby tried under that hood to recall a movie where the leading actress was tied and hooded by two madmen. She couldn't. She tried to think of one where the leading actress was rescued by her lover, but she couldn't do that either. She was hoping that by thinking about these things, her mind might relax some. But it didn't. There was one thing she knew. Her tied hands were causing her a lot of pain.

"I got a question," Abby said.

"Well, well, what is it Miss? What can I help you with?" Luther said.

"Can you please loosen my hands? They are hurting. Please?"

"I'll sure see about her, Clyde. We sure want to make her comfortable now, don't we? She's our guest."

He got up from the sofa and walked to Abby.

Luther adjusted the electrical cord that they had wrapped around her wrist making it tighter still. Abby moaned sharply.

"Is that better sweetie? Do you feel better now?"

Then he cupped both her breasts with his hands and squeezed down like he was making orange juice from oranges. She jerked tried to jerk away from him but couldn't.

*"You bastard! Get your hands off me!"*

"Oh, baby, all the purty girls like it this way. I know you do. I know you like it rough, baby."

"Now Luther, why'd you go and do that? That just ain't nice. You told me we were goin' to be nice. That's what you said, wasn't it? You told me that Luther."

"Goddamnit, Clyde, do I have to *keep* remindin' you who's in charge? I thought we'd gotten this straight? Don't you say another goddamn thing to me about her. You understand?"

Luther squeezed one final time and slapped Abby hard across her face. She said nothing. Luther walked into the kitchen and returned with roll of gray masking tape and taped Abby's mouth.

"Now, bitch, I don't have to hear another word from you."

"Luther, you're not hurtin' her are you?"

"Clyde, goddamnit, don't say another thing to me about this bitch. You got it?"

"I won't say another thing Luther. I promise you I won't. I promise."

"Good, goddamnit."

"You can count on me, Luther. You can always count on me to help."

"That's good, Clyde. Much better. Now I'm goin' to take a little nap, and when I wake up in a little while we'll deal with Missy Bitch the right way. You understand?"

"I understand, Luther. I always understand."

Luther got up from the sofa and walked into the cabin's only bedroom, but did not close the door. From inside the bedroom he could hear Clyde.

"Okay, Luther, you best get your rest. I'll take care of things out here. I won't let you down, Luther."

"I know you won't Clyde. You do your part and you can have some fun with her too. We both will."

Clyde didn't respond, but kept staring at Abby.

At that moment Abby wished she had finished the poem she had begun writing for her mother when she was standing over Homer Jones' tomato plants thinking about the love and gentleness of her mother, and her childhood memories. Her mind went back to her childhood. When she was a little girl, she thought everybody had a mother like hers. Later she learned differently. She thought she would never see her mother again. Never see anyone again. She remembered what she was going to name the poem: *My Mother's Hands*. She had written other poems for her mother, the first was when she was nine.

She thought it odd that at that moment the name had come back to her. She had not written it on her notepad, but she had planned to when she had finished writing each line. Before this day she had planned to do a lot of things.

She thought about something else after Luther had gone into the bedroom, leaving Clyde on the sofa to watch her. Thoughts of her own death and how it would happen in that cabin or in the woods or along the river were in her mind now, and could not be dislodged. What had been far beyond her thoughts before stopping at Homer's trailer was now ripping them apart much the way a gardener uses tools to spread the earth before planting. Things had changed.

# CHAPTER 14

With Lard riding in the front seat where Abby once was, I was driving from Camper's Haven to Sheriff Dupree's office in Cordele. We had spent more than thirty minutes riding and looking for Abby throughout Camper's Haven and knocking on a half-dozen doors asking people if they had seen her. Each time the answer was the same, "No."

"Where could she be? Where could she be? *Where could she be?*"

I had said those sentences like one of my scratched albums, stuck in the same spot and repeating itself. I had both hands on the steering wheel, but took my right one off and slapped the dashboard five times. I hit it a little harder each time.

"Hey, now, we'll find her," Lard said. "I'm going to help you. Feed a monkey and watch him shit. We'll find her. I promise you that, John. We'll find Abby."

I was thinking the worst and couldn't stop it. I had read enough and been a reporter long enough to know what sick, crazy, violent, mean, drunken, stupid sons-of-bitches are capable of. I had written enough crime stories to be reminded of that. I didn't want to be reminded of it, but I was. I tried to push all of it out of my mind, but wasn't able to. Exactly like one of my scratched records on the turntable. Bad thoughts kept repeating themselves. But who would want to do something terrible to Abby? And why?

"Maybe she's back there in one of those trailers we didn't knock on," Lard said. "Maybe someone invited her in and she was just getting out of the heat and time slipped by. Maybe that's *all* there is to this. Maybe she saw an old friend. Somebody she knows."

"That's not it, Lard. That isn't Abby. She's not going to leave her purse and book on the ground. She wouldn't have gone without telling me. She just wouldn't have. Something else is happening here."

"I reckon you're right. But we'll find her. I'll help you. I know we'll find her."

"Something bad has happened to her. I don't know what exactly, but it's bad, Lard."

"Don't think that way. Hell, man, Camper's Haven is the safest place in the world. Those are good folks in those trailers. This is God's country. Wherever she is, she's all right. There are good folks all around."

"Lard, didn't Tony Patrick get the ever-living shit kicked out of him a few weeks ago at your place? Did God do that? Or some of those *good folks* from God's country? He was probably run off the road the other night by somebody trying to kill him. He believes it anyway."

"You think somebody tried to run Tony off the highway? Is that what you think?"

"Yes, because that's what he thinks. That's what he told me and Abby when we saw him at the hospital."

"Well, shit a dead monkey a thousand times."

A few minutes later I pulled into the back parking lot of the courthouse and parked three spaces from a Crisp County sheriff's patrol car. We got out of the car and walked toward a silver metal door in the back, opened it, and walked down a dirty-smelling hall leading to the sheriff's department. There were several cigarette butts on the floor and in a small metal trashcan there were many white Styrofoam cups for coffee, and three empty packs of Red Man chewing tobacco. It reminded me of my first few months at the *Chronicle* and going to the Albany Police Department each morning covering the police beat. Coffee and tobacco and car-accident reports and robberies and shootings and domestic violence and rapists and murderers, and I had written about all of it. It didn't make me feel good thinking about it.

At the front desk of the sheriff's department was a woman wearing a powder blue wig big enough to hide a covey of quail. Mom and dad and four or five chicks. She had long red fingernails and was making them redder with her afternoon polishing. I bet she had polished them in the morning. The smell of polish slowed my breathing. The woman was chewing Spearmint gum fast, mechanically fast. If there had been a world championship for gum chewing, she would've won the title. She was smoking a cigarette and flipped her ashes in a large ashtray inscribed: The Georgia Sheriffs' Association.

From her polishing she looked up and saw us walking in fast. I was about five steps ahead of Lard.

"Morning, hun, what can I do for y'all?"

"I need to report a missing person," I said. "Her name's Abby Sinclair, she's from Albany and works for the *Albany Chronicle*. I don't know where she is."

She put down her fingernail brush and picked up her cigarette and took a long pull that reminded me of the way Mickey smoked in the newsroom. The woman turned her head to the right and exhaled a thick cloud that covered her powder blue wig.

"Is that right? A missin' person. I don't remember ever havin' one of those, hun. Been here thirteen years."

I was headed past her through double metal doors to where the sheriff and his deputies worked. She stopped me.

"Hold up right there, hun. Let me call Sheriff Dupree or one of his deputies. You just can't run on back there unannounced. That wouldn't be proper, now would it? The Big Man don't like that. No, he doesn't."

The woman took another long pull from her cigarette. She turned to the left this time, and blew smoke toward the ceiling. She kept popping her gum. Then she picked up her black telephone and punched three numbers and spoke.

"Sheriff, I got two men out here in a big, big hurry. One says he's here to report a missin' person. Never had one of those have we?"

The woman listened for five seconds.

"Yes, sir, I will. Okay, Sheriff. I'll tell 'im."

She hung up the telephone and looked at me.

"Can we go?" I said. "Can we go now? I need to see the Sheriff."

"Easy there, hun, the Sheriff says he'll see you right away. He'll help y'all. He helps everyone. He said y'all can go on back right now.

Don't have to wait. "

She pressed a button under her gray metal desk, and the two doors behind her slowly opened.

"Thank you, ma'am," I said.

"And thank you again, ma'am," Lard said.

"You boys go right on back there now. Big Man – I mean *Sheriff Dupree* – will help you find whoever you're lookin' for. I know he will. He's a good man."

She put her cigarette in the ashtray and picked up her fingernail brush. She looked down and resumed polishing her nails. She was focused on them.

I walked first through the double doors with Lard a few steps behind. I saw the sheriff's office with Dupree's door opened, and we walked in. Cigar smoke was thick in his office. He could've had deputies hiding in the corners and we couldn't have seen them. The cigar was as big as an ear of corn. Dupree was in a large black leather chair behind one of the biggest desks for a lawman, or any man, I had ever seen. It was shiny wood, and probably cost as much as the annual salary of the woman with the powder blue wig. Behind Dupree's desk hung a plaque indicating he had recently been selected Georgia's Lawman of the Year by the state's Sheriffs' Association. There were lots of pictures on the walls covering his almost three decades as Crisp County's sheriff. He was smiling big in all of them.

He had a notebook opened in front of him, and when I saw it, I remembered Abby's that I had found by Homer's tomato plants. Dupree's thick, long cigar was in the left side of his mouth, but he took it out and pressed the lit part against a metal ashtray and put it out. The sheriff got up when we approached his desk.

"Howdy boys, I'm Sheriff Dupree. What can I do for you?"

He extended his hand to shake ours. He shook hands with each of us and sat back down in the big chair behind his desk.

"Boys, have a seat so I can take down everything you need to tell me. I want to do everything I can to help y'all."

We sat down in two uncomfortable metal-back chairs in front of Dupree's desk. I leaned forward with both hands on top of my knees. Lard sat back and looked around the room, and it was easier now to see everything in it since the cigar smoke was clearing. Dupree picked up a black ballpoint pen, and before he spoke, I did.

"I lost her at Homer's trailer not far from Lard's. He owns the Gator Pit on the Flint. We've been looking since then, and I just don't know where she is. Her name is Abby Sinclair and she works for the *Albany Chronicle* and she lives in. . ."

"Son, slow down, son. I want to help you find whoever it is you've lost, but let's back up a bit here, boys. Let's start with a name and description. I want to get it all down. I can't remember the last time I had a missing person case. Must've been years ago."

I slowed my thoughts and words, but kept my hands on my knees in a ready position. Ready for what I didn't know. I took a long deep breath, much like I did before shooting a free throw the way my father had taught me. I started over and gave Dupree what he wanted. I started with Abby's full name, age, and then a physical description and then I told him that Abby lived in Albany and worked with me at the *Albany Chronicle*. Dupree asked a few questions and wrote in his notepad as I answered. It all took about ten minutes.

"Yes, sir, son, I did recognize your name right off. That's *fine* work you been doin' up here tryin' to get those folks at Transpower to clean up the mess they've made on our river. Tryin' to get them to do right. It's awful what they've done. My daddy took me fishing on the river when I was a boy. Did the same for my son. Just a shame. Just a shame. Keep up the good work."

He nodded his head and looked at me. He asked one more question about Abby's physical appearance and the clothes she was wearing, and wanted to know why we were at Homer Jones' trailer. All standard questions for a missing person investigation, I thought. I repeated a few things.

"I wanted to talk to Homer about the story I've been working on up here. He lives at Camper's Haven and he fishes, and I was told he could help me with my story. Abby was with me. She's my photographer. We talked to Lard, I mean Bubba Jackson, before going to Homer's trailer."

"Yes, sir, I know Homer," Dupree said. "He's a fine man and works here at the courthouse. I've known him for many years, and his family too. They good *colored* people. He lost his wife Melva to cancer a while back. She was a fine, fine Christian woman. Good colored people. The whole family."

"Yes sir, sheriff, I found that out too about Melva," I said. "Homer told me about her."

"Who told you to talk with Homer, son?"

"Willard Gentry."

"Well, another fine man. Both are good Christian men. Me and old Willard go back a heap of years, son. He's one of the best men around here. You can trust him all right. He's a real fine man, too."

He picked his cigar up and placed it in the left corner of his mouth. He did not re-light it. Dupree looked over our heads as if he was waiting for someone else to walk in his office. He didn't speak for several seconds.

"Anything else you need to know Sheriff?" I said.

"No, son, I think I got everything I need from you."

"Okay."

"Lard, anything I need from you? I know all about you and your store. Most folks in these parts do. You run a fine business."

"No, sir, Sheriff Dupree. John covered it all. It's just like he said. We know you'll help us. I'm just here to help John. To do what I can."

"I'll be contacting the GBI and FBI if we have to. And I'll go ahead and share this information now with my deputies. Let them get right on it."

"Yes, sir, sheriff. Thanks," I said.

"So if you haven't seen Miss Abby Sinclair in twenty-four hours, you contact me, Mr. Maynard, and I'll alert the feds and the state boys. That's the way it works. Got it? If you don't see her in twenty-four hours, then she'll be declared missing by my office."

"I understand sheriff."

"Well now, son, don't you worry, we'll find your friend if we have to and get her back to you. I got some good deputies in my office, and they know folks all over Southwest Georgia who can help. But I bet she'll show up today. Probably saw a friend drive by and got in the car to visit for a while and time slipped away on her. That can happen to anybody."

"No, sir, that's not something Abby would've done," I said.

"Well, okay then. You let me know if you haven't seen her in twenty four hours."

"I promise you that."

Dupree stood up again and walked to the front of his desk. We stood up from our chairs.

"Thanks again, Sheriff Dupree," I said.

"Well, now, son, again let me say thanks to *you*."

"For what?"

"I appreciate all those stories about Transpower and what those SOBs are doing to our river. That's a real public service you and your paper are doin', and all the folks around here agree. I bet you're goin' get some kinda fancy award when this thing's over. Won't you?"

"Sheriff, I appreciate that, but I'm just doing my job."

"If we have to, we'll find your photographer friend. I'll tell you that right now." He placed his right hand on top of my left shoulder and patted it twice.

"I hope you will," I said, extending my hand to shake Dupree's. Lard did the same.

We walked out of the sheriff's personal office and through the double doors, then past the woman at the desk with shiny red fingernails and a blue wig to match. She was still popping gum and blowing smoke. Her ashtray overflowed with cigarette butts.

"Bye, hun. Come back and see us anytime."

"Thanks for your help," I said.

"Like I said, any time."

We walked again down the dirty hall and out into the parking lot and got into my car and headed back to the Gator Pit.

"He's a good lawman, and he'll do his best," Lard said. "Bin doin' for years and years."

"I hope he doesn't have to."

"Yeah, you're right. We'll find her, John. She'll show up today. I know she will."

"Yeah, you're right."

We were leaving Cordele and driving south onto Highway 300, back toward the river and lake. Back where we had last seen Abby.

# CHAPTER 15

I kept a tight grip on the steering wheel and thought about what Abby had said the first night she spent with me, drinking wine and listening to Bob Dylan and Van Morrison, and how much she loved the words from the poets and where they could take her or anybody else who was willing to listen in full. Words were what she loved. Words properly spoken. They were as intoxicating to her as the wine we were drinking that night.

Maybe this was it for us, I thought. There'd be no more words together, no more music, no poetry or books to read and talk about. No more love-making. Only people crying and flowers everywhere at the funeral. Lots of flowers.

How the damn hell do all those missing person stories end anyway? I knew the answer to that question. I followed the news and read papers from all over the country that were mailed to the *Chronicle*. All those missing person stories ended without the person. They all ended badly. Missing hell, somebody knows where Abby is, and the ones who do shouldn't, while the ones who should, don't. Somebody took her and they're going to do terrible things to her that children, and adults, should not be told of. I tried to stop thinking this way, but the whole thing was gnawing at my gut like a hungry animal eating my insides. Abby being gone from me this way was making my whole body ache. The hurt was growing worse. None of the missing person stories ever ended well, the thought kept moving through my mind as if it were on a racetrack. How to stop it? I wanted off the track. I drove on with both hands on the wheel.

"Lard, do you want me to take you back to your store or somewhere else? I appreciate you going with me. This means a lot to me."

"My truck's there remember?"

"Yeah, that's right."

"Let's go back to the Pit. I didn't miss any business. I ain't had much to miss there lately, and you sure as hell know why. It's because of Transcrewed. Isn't that what Tony calls those bastards?"

"Yeah, that's it. That's what he calls them."

"My man Tony tells it like it is, like it was, and like it's always goin' to be. Feed a monkey and watch him shit. Just take me back to Camper's Haven and the Pit."

"At least Tony's all right now, but I'll never see Abby again. I just don't think I'll ever see her again."

"Hey, hey, hey, man, now don't start that kind of talk. She'll be found, and she'll be all right. I'll do whatever it takes. We'll find her. I'll help you."

"Lard, thanks. I got to stop thinking the way I'm thinking. I've got to try and stop it. It's killing me inside. We got to find her."

"Yeah, just stop it then. We'll find her. She'll be back."

I rubbed my forehead with the back of my left hand moving it hard back and forth several times while keeping my right hand on the steering wheel. Then I saw a group of buzzards eating a dead armadillo on the side of the road. The animals had not been there on our way to Cordele, I remembered. There were five big birds eating at the same time with fresh bright red blood on the asphalt.

It was about five-thirty that afternoon when we returned to Camper's Haven and the Gator Pit. It had been around three hours since I had last seen Abby. Since she had been taken. I drove through Camper's Haven as I had before, looking to my right for five seconds and then back to my left. Lard was doing the same. She was still out there looking at Homer's tomato plants, maybe, just maybe she was. She was not. I had her purse, notepad, and the book of poetry. I had placed in all in the backseat of my car.

I stopped in front of Homer Jones' trailer and looked at the last spot on this earth that I had seen her. I rolled down my window as if that would make her come back to me. I heard the humming of Homer's air conditioning and nothing more. I kept the window down for a minute, rolled it back up, and drove away from Homer's to the Gator Pit. I parked and we got out of my car.

Tony Patrick was standing at the front door of the Gator Pit. He had just driven into Camper's Haven, and it was the first time he had ever been locked out of the Pit in the middle of a summer afternoon. The stitches in his face and head had been removed, but there were visible scars on his face. He still had the cast on his right arm. The scars made him look like a character out of a horror movie.

"Trick or treat, boys, and I don't want any damn candy, either. I need a cold, cold beer, or I'll put a curse on you that'll last a thousand years."

Tony's joke evoked no emotion from us.

"Come on boys, I know I'm ugly, but I'm just having a little fun. I've got to keep laughing. I can't let this get to me. The scars will get better. That's what the docs say. Don't you want to kiss me?"

"Tony, you look like hell, but we got a bad situation here," Lard said. "Real bad. Shit-awful bad. Feed a monkey bad."

"How could it be worse than my face?"

"A few hours ago John was inside Homer Jones' trailer talking to him. That's when we lost her. She's missing. Taken. We don't know where she is."

"Taken? What the hell you mean, taken? Missing? Who's missing?"

"Abby," I said. "She's missing, Tony. We don't know where she is."

"What do you mean missing?" Tony said.

"That's what I mean," I said. "Just what I mean. Missing."

"Like John said, we don't know where she is, Tony," Lard said.

"We just got back from filing a missing person report with Sheriff Dupree," I said. "She's gone. I was inside about to interview Homer. I had gotten a tip from Willard Gentry to talk to Homer. Abby stayed outside to look at Homer's tomato plants, and I went inside Homer's trailer for a few minutes and came out to get her and she was gone. Nothing left but her purse, notepad, and a book of poems. She was gone, Tony."

"Tomato plants? What the hell is all of this about?" Tony said. "What do you mean missing? She's got be somewhere."

"Yeah, Tony, everybody's somewhere," Lard said. "We just don't know where Abby is."

"Yeah, tomatoes," I said. "She said they reminded her of her mother's. Like I said, I had just been inside a few minutes and then went back outside to get her, thinking she was probably getting too hot. She wasn't there."

"This don't make any sense," Tony said.

"Neither does your scarred-up face," Lard said. "A lot of things around here don't make any sense anymore."

"Yeah, he's right," I said.

"John, I'm sorry, man," Tony said. "What can I do to help? We'll find her. She'll be okay. We can find her."

I turned and looked toward the river and saw an osprey fly from the water's edge with a large fish in its beak. The bird flew to a nest in a cypress tree and gave the fish to two younger birds. I could see the smaller birds begin eating the fish as the large osprey flew away. I was transfixed on the birds for a few moments until I heard the sound of Lard's key chain.

Lard unlocked the front door of the Gator Pit and the three of us walked inside and sat down in short wooden chairs around a dark brown folding card table in the middle of the room. When business was slow, Lard, Tony, and other river men and women played cards, drank beer, and told stories around the table. On top of the table was a copy of the *Chronicle* that had the front-page story I had written after Tony had taken me on the initial boat ride when I saw and smelled how terrible the river was. That trip had put a sick feeling in my gut. What I had in my gut now was worse.

I turned the newspaper over so I wouldn't see the story or my by-line. The hell with that damn story and all the others about this goddamn river, I thought. Abby would be where she should be if not for that story. It was my fault. All my fault.

"You boys want a cold beer?" Lard said.

"No, thanks," I said.

"Me neither, Lard," Tony said.

"Hell, I don't want one either," Lard said. "I thought I'd ask. It don't sound good no ways. Does it?"

"No. Nothing does," I said.

Lard got up from the table and walked to the double-door glass cooler where he kept his beer and other drinks. He took three twelve-ounce Cokes from the cooler and returned to the table and sat down. He opened all three and passed one to Tony and me without asking. We all took a drink at the same time and set our cans down on the table. Several moments passed without a word being spoken. We took a second drink before anyone spoke.

"Tony, you look a lot better than the last time I saw you," I said. "When Abby and I came to see you in the hospital. You sure looked awful then."

"I'm doing a lot better," Tony said. "Don't worry about me buddyro. We got to, the three of us, figure out what we can do to find her. And we will find her. You say you saw the sheriff?"

"Yeah, Lard was with me."

"So they're lookin' for her," Tony said.

"If she doesn't show up in twenty four hours they will be," I said. "She's not going to show up. Somebody's got her. But why?"

"You know I don't trust anybody in that damn sheriff's office," Tony said.

"I know, Tony," I said, "and I know why. Lard knows now. I told him what you told Abby and me about Luther's car that night."

"Tony, you believe it was Luther's car that ran you off the road?" Lard said.

"I know it was. No doubt in my mind, and whoever was driving it wanted me dead. Maybe the same folks got Abby. They haven't gotten me and now they're tryin' someone else."

"Feed a monkey and watch him shit." Lard said.

"I was almost a dead monkey that night," Tony said.

I flipped the *Chronicle* over and over. Took a drink of Coke and stood up from the table.

"I can't sit here," I said. "I've got to do something. Should I call her mother? I don't know Abby's mother. She told me her name, but I can't remember it. What the hell am I going to do? Should I call Mickey and let the paper know?"

"Easy, John," Tony said. "This shit is hard and it's now gotten real hard. But let's think a minute about you and Abby and what happened before you went into Homer's trailer. Let's just take a minute."

"What is there to think about?" I said.

"Where were you before going to Homer's?" Tony said. "Where were you?"

"Feed a monkey, watch him shit, Tony, they came into the Pit to get directions. Don't you remember John, we saw those two asshole deputies pull up in the parking lot and haul ass away. Don't you remember?"

"Yeah, Lard. I remember them."

"What deputies? Crisp County boys?" Tony said.

"Yep, Clyde Ferrell and Luther Wright," Lard said. "They was off duty and driving that big Buick that Luther has. The one you said tried to kill you."

"Well, those *bastards!*" Tony said.

I sat in the chair again and turned full to Tony. It was like someone had shocked me with jumper cables.

"Tony, you still believe that?" I said. "You still certain about what happened that night when you left the Opry Barn? You still believe it was Luther's car?"

"You better damn well believe it. I know what I saw."

"*Son-of-a-bitch!*" I said.

I stood up again from my chair.

"Yeah, Tony, I've been wondering about that myself since John told me," Lard said. "Are you God-Almighty positive it was Luther Wright's car that night? We just saw the sumbitch."

"I told you I was certain that it was Luther's car that ran me off the road. I couldn't tell who was it, but, by God, I know it was his car. I've seen it a thousand times. All over this damn county."

Now Tony stood up from the table.

"And that car was here today about the same time me and Abby were here. Right Lard?"

"Yeah, that was Luther's car. I know it was. No doubt about it."

"You know what this means don't you, Tony?" I said.

"You're damn right I do."

I reached again for the newspaper, picked it up and rolled it as a newspaper boy would who was about to make his morning delivery. I held it close to my face before tapping it five times on the table. Then I dropped it on the table.

"Do you really think so?" I said. "Same car?"

"I bet we're right, Mr. Big Shot Reporter," Tony said. "I know what you're thinking."

"I know what you're thinking," I said.

"Will somebody tell me what anybody's thinking?" Lard said.

"Lard, it's the deputies," I said. "The Crisp County deputies. It's them and we got to find them. They got Abby. They tried to kill Tony. We got to find where they are. We find them, we find Abby."

"Crazy-ass Luther Wright's got Abby?" Lard said. "He tried to kill Tony?"

"They took Abby and they tried to kill me that night after I left the Opry Barn," Tony said. "That's exactly what we're saying."

There was silence in the Gator Pit with Tony and me looking at each other nodding our heads in agreement, and Lard scratching his head as if there was something on it he couldn't get off.

"Well, feed the monkey and watch him shit," Lard said. "Maybe you boys are right."

"We ain't got time to a feed a monkey," Tony said. "I don't know where he lives, but we got to find him. We find Luther. We find Abby."

"Where's he live, where's he live?" I said. "Lard, do you *know*?"

"Luther? Luther Wright?"

"Yeah, Luther Wright," I said. "Sheriff Dupree's deputy. We've got to find him. We got to go now, Lard. *Now!*"

Lard stood up from the chair, and I leaned into him as if I was going to fall on top of him. He took three steps back. I kept leaning and now was three inches from his face. I needed answers.

"Whoa now!" Lard said. "You need to calm down a bit."

"Tell me where he lives, Lard," I said. "I've got to get there."

"You really think he took Abby?" Lard said. "I don't. I been knowin' Luther Wright for years and he may be a catfish turd, but he ain't doin' stuff like that. He's a piss ant all right, but not a kidnapper. He wouldn't try to kill somebody or take somebody. No, sir. Not

Luther. He ain't a kidnapper. He ain't a killer."

"He may have taken Abby or maybe not," Tony said. "I know for damn sure it was his old brown Buick that ran me off the road, and it's what you saw here today not long before she was gone. Right, Lard?"

"Yeah, damn sure was his car today, and he was in it."

"Lard, tell us where he lives," I said. "*Now, damn it!*"

"Okay, okay. He has a cabin at the End of the Line. It's in the woods not far from the Flint. It'll take us a few minutes to get there."

"We're all at the end of the line," I said. "What do you mean?"

"No, no, now listen to me," Lard said. "The End of the Line is an old loggin' access road along the river a few miles over yonder. He's got a cabin there. A few years ago I used to be a regular at their poker games. Sheriff Dupree used to show up. I quit goin' when the sheriff kept winnin'. I think he kept aces in his gun holster."

Lard pointed north and out the window where we had earlier that day seen the car come into the parking lot, turn up dust, and speed away. Luther Wright's car. Maybe the one someone put Abby in.

"Can you get us there?" I said.

"Yeah, I still remember the way. I can get us there."

# CHAPTER 16

I was again behind the steering wheel of my car. Tony got into the front seat and Lard in the back. I sped away from the Gator Pit and dust from the road filtered into the trees lining the road out of Camper's Haven. I was going fifty over Alligator Lane, and each hole I hit created enough force in the backseat to bounce Lard from one spot to another. He was the biggest jack-in-the-box in Georgia.

"Hold on there, cowboy! My fat ass is flyin' everywhere back here! You're killin' me back here."

I went faster.

"You go as fast as you can," Tony said. "Don't listen to him. He'll be all right."

"I've got to get there, Tony," I said. "We've got to get there. If you and I are right, we'll get her out of there. We'll take care of her. We'll get her back."

"I'm with you all the way," Tony said.

"Me too, John. But you're killin' me back here. You're goin' to have to slow down some."

I hit the brakes at the end of the dirt road coming out of Camper's Haven and away from the last place I had seen Abby. When I stopped at the stop sign, I realized I didn't know the way to Luther's cabin.

"Lard, talk to me big man, talk to me!" I said. "Which way is it? How do we get there?"

Lard gave me directions that would take us down a paved county road, past a couple of subdivisions with fine homes and trucks and boats in their yards, and then on to a series of dirt roads running mainly due north parallel with the Flint River. He figured it was about eight or nine miles from the Gator Pit. He said he knew the land well and remembered one hunting trip there a few years ago where he shot a ten-point buck that weighed around two hundred pounds. That trip was a lot of fun. This one wasn't going to be that way.

I sped from the stop sign after Lard gave me directions. My old car rattled its way again and this time to around sixty miles an hour. A crow flew overhead toward green peanut fields. The sun was beginning its descent, sliding beyond the fields and the trees in the distance.

"You better pull back on her some, John," Tony said. "I can't imagine what you're feelin'. It would be the same for me if it was Rebecca and not Abby, but you keep this up and we'll be pulled over by cops before we find the cops."

"If we're right Tony, there's two fewer cops on these roads tonight."

I slowed my car and looked at Tony then re-focused on the road.

"You're probably right," Tony said.

Now the sun was a red ball sitting over a row of rusted-silver irrigation pipes, like a giant octopus installed in the fields over corn and soybeans. Above the car, a mockingbird was pestering a crow. That small mockingbird was relentless. It chased the big crow over the octopus toward the fading sun. I remembered Abby and I had seen the same kind of bird scene earlier.

"You're going to have to turn here," Lard said. "This here road will take us where we need to go. We're not far now."

Lard pointed to another dirt road. We left behind the seemingly orderly homes of a subdivision. I drove on.

"We got to get there," I said. "That's where she is. It has to be."

Two miles down this road I saw an old green metal sign, tilted almost parallel to the ground as if it had been there a long time and no one had taken care of it. *The End of the Line* was hand-written on the sign. I followed Lard's instructions and turned onto the road.

The narrow red dirt road was lined with pines and occasional oaks, and thick in some parts where the trees formed a canopy keeping out sunlight all day. Next, I drove by a wooden shack old enough, it seemed, for a nineteenth-century sharecropping family. Outside, two black boys, about nine or ten, were spraying each other with a long black water hose. They seemed happy and smiled with white teeth showing clear against their black skin. Near the boys was an old, green John Deere tractor and sleeping under it was a long, brown hound dog with ears to the ground. It looked like one of the dogs I had seen under Homer Jones' trailer earlier that day when Abby was with me.

The End of the Line took us over a railroad track no longer used for trains and deeper into the piney woods away from scattered homes where farm hands and their families lived. Now there was nothing but forest and fields, where cotton and peanuts had been planted, where deer and turkey lived. The Flint River was not far away.

"How far, Lard?" I said. "How far now?"

"Hell, son, I reckon all the way to the End of the Line. We ain't got much farther to go. This here road is about to play out. You just hang on and we'll see that cabin in just a minute or two. Feed a monkey. We'll all see it, I promise you that."

A red-tailed hawk flew over my car and into the ditch on the driver's side, and came out of it with a large gray rat in his claws. Dinner seemed to come easy. The road was curving sharply to the right and along each side were trees, and thick green and brown underbrush. Darkness was coming.

"Stop here, John," Lard said. "Stop here. We'll walk from here. Park over here on the side of the road. Luther's cabin is only a bit up there. You can't see it, but I know it's there."

Lard said the cabin was a few hundred yards away. He raised his right hand and used his index finger and pointed to what we had come for, but couldn't see it.

"If you boys are right, she's in there," Lard said. "I still don't believe crazy Luther would do something this crazy. I still don't believe it."

"I hope we are right, Lard," Tony said. "All you got to do is help us get her out of there. She's in there. I bet she is. They tried to kill me and now they took her."

"Feed a monkey, watch him shit, boys. I'll do what we have to, you boys know that."

I pulled off to the right side of the road near a large pecan orchard adjacent to the cabin. The cabin was still not in view. Now the sun had disappeared. We got out of the car and ran about fifty yards into the orchard. Lard ran fast, but was about ten yards behind Tony and me. We stopped behind a large tree and out of sight from anyone driving on End of the Line. From the tree I could see the cabin was about two football fields away. The night kept coming. Darkness now filled the orchard. Clouds had moved over the land, blocking the stars above.

We were breathing fast and hard and looking around the orchard and toward the cabin, and around the orchard and at the cabin again. We saw no one. There were no drivers on the road. We heard crickets from the woods and bullfrogs from a nearby pond used for irrigation. It was the same as it ever was. A few moments passed, and we began to breathe easier. We said nothing for several moments. The talking was done by animals. We kept looking all around. Finally Tony spoke.

"What's your plan now, Mr. Reporter?"

"I thought you had one," I said. "You're the man with the big ideas. I just write them down."

"Now feed a monkey, boys," Lard said. "Someone's got to have a plan! I sure as hell don't. One of you smart-asses needs to come up with somethin'."

"I don't have a plan for this thing," Tony said. "I'm not good at sneakin' up on cops and beatin' the hell out of them. And rescuing women. I'm good at other things."

"Just remember how they beat the hell out of you and I'm sure you'll do fine," I said.

I looked at Tony, then at Lard, and back toward the cabin. I could see lights from inside the cabin, and I could see what appeared to be Luther's car parked in front of it.

Tony grabbed my right arm and pulled me close to him. He looked at me as a father might a young son who was about to hear that something awful had just happened to his family. Something the father didn't want to say.

"I don't know what were going to find in there. It could be something real..."

I didn't let him finish what he was saying.

"I've got to get in there. I've got to find her and get her away from here, and that's what we're going to do, Tony."

"Let's get this thing movin' before somebody sees us out here," Lard said. "We want to see them first. What's our plan? We need a plan."

"Stop worrying about it, Lard. It'll come to us," I said.

"*When?*" Tony said.

"Let's go!" I said.

"What?" Lard said.

"I said let's go. Follow me."

I broke from the tree and ran toward the cabin, with Tony and Lard running behind me. As we got closer to the cabin I could see a black Ford pickup truck parked under a white aluminum shelter near the cabin. From the pecan tree we had hidden behind, we had not been able to see the truck or the singlewide white trailer behind the cabin. Now we could clearly see it all as we ran toward the cabin. The crickets were louder. We ran about seventy-five yards and stopped behind another pecan tree. All was calm. I saw no movement through the windows of the cabin. I saw no movement outside the cabin. Everything had come into full view. Everything, I thought, but a plan to find out if Abby was in there, and how to get her out if she was.

"Wait, wait, wait a damn minute," Tony said. "I'll be a dirty damn *son-of-a-bitch*! That truck belongs to Sheriff Dupree. I know it. I've seen him get out of it several times at Stripling's Diner. I've seen him in it all over the county. That's his. So he's come out for a little social visit with his deputies. They all may be in there with her. They may all be in this thing together."

"We got to get Abby out of there," I said. "I don't care who all is in there. We're going to get her out."

"We don't know she's in there," Lard said. "We could all be wrong about this. Like I said, I don't think Luther is this big of an asshole. You boys may be wrong."

"Hell, yeah, she's in there," Tony said. "I know what ran me off the road that night. It all makes sense. These boys are trying to stop John and stop me and stop Abby. It has to be about the river, it's all about the river. What else could it be?"

"It has to be," I said. "It's all the same. Why would they take Abby? What else could it be?"

"What else could it be?" Lard said.

"Nothing else," Tony said.

Tony shook his head fast from side to side a few times like a boy who just took his first shot of Jack Daniels.

"Let's move, damn it," Lard said. "Tell me what you want me to do. Let's get out of these trees and to that cabin. We got to know for sure she's in there."

"I'm ready," Tony said.

"Me, too," I said.

I looked at Lard with sweat dripping off his nose onto his overalls. Then I looked at Tony and the scars on his face, like red lines on a road map. I thought of her a final time.

"*Let's go!*" I said.

I ran from the safety of the pecan tree to the trailer behind the cabin. Tony and Lard followed me one more time. We made it to the trailer and hid behind it with Luther's cabin in front of the trailer. Woods were all around us and the river nearby. There we waited for a few moments. We wouldn't wait long.

"*What if you're wrong?*" I said. "*What if I'm wrong?*"

Tony whispered back.

"*We'll say we came over for a poker game. But we won't have to. She's in there. Abby's in there.*"

"*I hope so,*" I said.

The cabin's back door opened and Clyde Ferrell walked out with a large black trash bag full of empty beer cans, empty liquor bottles, and empty Kentucky Fried Chicken boxes. Clyde was walking toward two gray metal trash barrels that were between his trailer, and the black Ford pickup. Sheriff Dupree's truck. Clyde looked up at the sky when he walked. Crickets were louder now with the buzzing of other insects, too. Abby would've called it "beautiful music of the land, and for the people who live on it." Her momma said it that way, she said.

"*If you believe, now's the time,*" Tony said.

Before I could speak, Lard did in a whisper.

"*Stay here both of you. I'll tell you when to come.*"

I was going to reply, but didn't, as I saw Lard lower his head as a fullback does carrying the football, and run as fast as he could to the near side of the trailer. Once at the trailer, Tony and I could see Lard walk to the other side of it where the trash barrels were. Then we lost sight of him.

Lard walked as a man does when he has something important he wants to see and think about. He saw Clyde. The deputy had removed the metal lid from one of the trash barrels, and was about to drop the black bag in. Clyde was looking into the barrel.

"Hey, Clyde. How you doing tonight? It sure is pretty out here ain't it? It's been a while since I been out here. You remember I used to come and play poker with you boys? You remember, don't you Clyde?"

Clyde dropped the bag on the ground. He dropped the lid too. He pissed in his pants, a long stream that went warm down his right leg. Clyde had a look of fear and dread. Like a baby rabbit in the clutches of a red-tailed hawk. It was a few moments before he was able to speak.

"Lard, shit, damn, hell, Lard! Ya 'bout scared all the livin' piss out of me. Why'd you do that?"

"Well, maybe not all of it," Lard said, looking at the wet spot on Clyde's pants.

Even in the twilight, Lard could see Clyde's red face of embarrassment. It was as red as the Budweiser cans in the trash bag.

"What, what, what are you doing out here?" Clyde said. "Why'd you sneak up on me like that?"

"I was out driving and my truck broke down back a ways. Damn thing just stopped on me. Don't that just piss you off when that happens, Clyde?"

"I reckon it does."

"Can you help me?"

Clyde didn't answer but leaned over to pick up the empty beer cans and chicken boxes that had fallen out of the trash bag. He put all the trash in the trash barrel. It took him only a few seconds, and after he was through he stood up fully again. Then he went back down again. All the way flat this time.

Lard had swung with his right arm, extended long, and with his fist he caught Clyde underneath his jaw. Lard was concerned that whoever was in the cabin could hear the punch. It was solid. Blood trickled out of Clyde's mouth and nose. When Clyde saw the punch coming, it was already over for him. Clyde was out. Flat on his back. Lard looked at him for a moment. Clyde wasn't moving. The blow produced little blood. Not like the night Tony was forced off the highway in his car and slammed against a pecan tree. There was plenty of blood that night. Nor the night Tony was attacked at the Gator Pitt. Lot more blood both times.

Clyde was still as a piece of cordwood when Lard grabbed his ankles and pulled him behind the trailer out of view from anyone who was in the cabin. Lard ran back to the side of the trailer closest to Tony and me. And there he waved for us. We saw the signal and came running. We came low and fast out of the pecan orchard to where Lard was standing over Clyde. We came unseen by whoever might be in the cabin.

I looked down at Clyde and thought he had a slight smile on his face and that whatever Lard had done to him was something that might've helped him. He looked peaceful despite the trickle of blood on his chin and under his nose.

"You didn't kill him did you Lard?" Tony said.

"No, feed a damn monkey, I didn't kill the boy, but he'll take a nice nap for a spell. He needed a long rest anyway. Don't you think?"

"Probably did," Tony said.

"Fine job, Lard," I said.

"Feed a monkey, I liked doin' it."

I looked at the singlewide trailer and saw that no lights were on, and walked up the back steps and opened the door. I went in and turned a light on and a minute later came out with a brown extension cord, a dishtowel, and a roll of black electrical tape all of which I found in separate kitchen drawers. I came back to where Clyde was lying on the ground and turned him over on his side, pulled his arms behind his back, and tied his ankles and arms together using the extension cord. Clyde moaned twice and stopped. Then I put the dishtowel around his mouth and taped it tight using the electrical tape, wrapping it six times around his head. I did not cover his nose with the towel.

"Damn, John, you done this before ain't you?" Lard said.

"Nope, first time."

"I don't believe it," Tony said.

"Let's go!" I said. "Follow me now."

I eased around the trailer under the cover of darkness with Tony and Lard behind me. As we turned the corner of the trailer near the black truck, we heard the back door of the cabin open and ran low behind the trash barrel into a row of scrub pines and a blackberry thicket. We waited there, and our breathing was low. We were motionless.

"Damn it, Clyde where are you?" Luther said. "I told you to get some beer and come right back. We got things to do in here. Hurry up, goddamnit! Miss purty bitch misses you. She wants you. She wants both of us."

He slammed the door and went back inside and was cussing all the while.

"Where is that sumbitch. That sumbitch better get in here in now."

"Now let's move," I said.

We ran to the back of the cabin near the door that Luther had just opened. We stopped with our backs pressed against the brown logs with a sweet resin smell, but we didn't wait long.

"Lard, I want you to come into the cabin through the backdoor," I said, "but not until you here my signal. You got it?"

"What signal?" Lard said.

"You'll know it," I said. "Just listen hard and when you hear it don't waste time."

"This all sounds so simple," Lard said.

"Tony, I'm going through the front door and I need you with me," I said. "She's in there and we can't wait any longer. We don't know what that crazy bastard's going to do."

"I'm with you," Tony said.

Tony and I left Lard at the back of the cabin and, with bodies crouched, we trotted around the other side of the cabin near the front porch. We were behind a row of green boxwood plants with the brown Buick parked next to the wooden steps. We heard voices from inside.

# CHAPTER 17

"They ain't gonna give us the rest of the money," one man said. "They done told me that. They're pretty pissed at us right now for screwin' this thing up so far."

"Boss, me and Clyde did everything you asked," another man said. "We been doin' our best to make this thing right. I swear Boss."

"I didn't tell you stupid sumbitches to take this damn girl, now did I?" the first man said.

There was a minute's pause before another word was spoken. We were crouched still at the boxwoods in front of the cabin. The clouds had gone, and the night sky was beginning to fill with stars. A half moon was visible. More talk came from inside.

"No, but we figured this would work," the second man said. "Nothing else was workin', Boss. Nothin' was workin'."

"*Holy Jesus Son of God!*" the first man said. "She knows you now. She knows both of you. You were callin' each other by name when I got here. I heard you when I got out of my truck. If she knows you two, that'll lead to me. You've really messed this thing up, Luther, goddamnit. You and Clyde really screwed up this time."

"She ain't seen us, Boss," Luther said. "I promise you that. She ain't seen us. I figured this was how we could stop it all, since we didn't do it that night on the highway. I thought it was over then, but it wasn't. We tried our best, me and Clyde did. We always try our best for you, Boss."

"Luther, your best ain't good enough this time."

"We tried, Boss," Luther said. "We tried for you just like we always do."

"Yeah, but this tonight don't make piss ant sense," Boss said.

"I'm tellin' you this thing is over. It's over! Now I got to figure out what to do with this little girl. I guess we got to end it here. Right here tonight."

"Yeah, Boss, I know."

"Well, goddamnit, let's get it done."

"Okay, Boss."

"Now."

Voices stopped for a few moments, and I heard movement from inside the cabin. Someone was walking toward the front door. Tony and I held still.

"I wonder what that slow sumbitch Clyde is doing," Luther said. "I wanted him to take care of her, if that's what you want done, Boss. What the hell's takin' him so long? He was supposed to take out the trash, get some beer, and get my pistol out of my car, but I guess I will now."

The front cabin door opened and Luther Wright walked onto the porch and down the steps. Before his right black boot hit the final step, I latched on to it like an alligator attacking a duck, and pulled his leg toward the rising moon. Luther came crashing down hitting his head on the wooden steps. After Luther had been up-ended and was lying on the front porch motionless, Tony opened the Buick and found the gun in the glove compartment. He took the thirty-eight caliber pistol from the car. Then two minutes later the cabin door opened a second time.

Sheriff Dupree had turned the porch light on and walked onto the porch and looked down at Luther.

"Well, goddamnit, you can't even walk outside without screwing everything up, can you now? Now get your ass up and get your gun. We're goin' to take care of this girl. I know no other way."

Luther didn't move or say anything. Tony and I had backed away from the porch, and out of Dupree's sight.

"Lard! Lard! Lard! Now!" I hollered.

Lard burst through the back door and ran fast through the cabin's den, and saw Abby sitting in the straight-back chair with her hands tied, the black hood still over her face and mouth taped shut.

He did not stop.

Sheriff Dupree turned around and saw Lard charging through the cabin and toward him like a bull. Dupree had no time to play matador. Lard shot through the screen door and his head hit the sheriff square in his chest. Lard wrapped his arms around him in a form tackle that would've pleased any college football coach. The force of the hit carried Lard and Sheriff Dupree off the porch onto the gravel driveway where the Buick was parked. They had flown over Luther who was still lying backside on the porch. When they hit the driveway, the sheriff groaned and was motionless. Lard then sat on Dupree's midsection with his legs across the sheriff's chest. He contained the sheriff as he once did an alligator.

Tony was standing over Luther and pointing his thirty-eight caliber pistol at him. Luther was shaking his head slightly, beginning to move his body some. Luther had the look of a drunk about to begin a long hangover. Sheriff Dupree had the look of a man caught by his wife in bed with another woman. He wished things were going to be that simple.

"Well, well, this here sumbitch doesn't wiggle near as much as old Mr. Gator did," Lard said. "I believe I can stay on this one all night long. What do you say sheriff? Is this goin' to be good for you? It's sure good for me."

"Don't you worry about that gator," Tony said. "He ain't goin' nowhere. I think he likes it when you're on top. It's good to him that way."

Tony moved his aim from Luther to the sheriff and to Luther again. Then back to the sheriff. Tony walked over to Luther.

"Keep your ass right there. Don't you move one bit."

He held the gun over Luther, who didn't move.

I went into the cabin, and there she was. I took the tape from her mouth, pulled the hood off her head and her face was red and swollen from being slapped. Her shirt was wet with sweat. She didn't know who it was that had removed her hood. I had said nothing. Then she saw me.

"I've been waiting, Robin Hood," Abby said. "I've been waiting. . ."

She began to cry. She tried to speak, but couldn't. She kept crying, loud and long sobs of pain. It was emotion she had contained since the moment she was taken at Homer's trailer. I did not try to stop her. I struggled to untie the electrical cord that bound her hands together behind her back, and went into the kitchen and found a sharp knife and cut it. Her arms were weak from being stretched and tied behind her. When the cord fell from her, she hugged me.

She kept crying, but not as loud as before. Her crying still had the same painful rhythm. We embraced and fell over onto the floor. Neither one said a word, or a part of a word, for a couple of minutes.

"Abby, I was going to find you," I said. "I was going to do whatever it took to find you. I was never not coming for you. Didn't you know? You had to know."

I felt a tear fall out of my right eye and onto my cheek. It rolled off my face onto the cabin floor.

She now smiled, and her crying stopped. A few moments later it started again, and I held tight to her as if someone or some awful thing was trying to pry us from one another. I wasn't going to let that happen. Finally, after a few more minutes, she begin to relax.

"John…John…John…"

"What? I'm right here, Abby. I'm right here."

"I love you, John. Even before all this. I love you, Johnny Boy."

"Abby, I feel the same. Even before all this."

"You do?"

"I love you. Yeah, before all of this."

"Well, Johnny Boy, you made it all good again. You saved me, and now I'm yours. Just like in your dreams."

"Just like."

She kissed me on the mouth. I began to help Abby off the floor and onto her feet, and heard the sound of a vehicle pulling into the driveway. Tony kept the gun in his hand guarding Sheriff Dupree and his deputy on the porch. They were going nowhere. Soon both of them and Clyde would be going somewhere for a long time.

# CHAPTER 18

Homer Jones had driven his truck to the cabin and parked and got out. He walked up the steps to the porch, and greeted both Lard and Tony. They spoke in return. No one seemed surprised to see him except Sheriff Dupree.

"Well, you don't need my help looks like," Homer said. "It seems what's done has been done here. I guess old Dupree will get somethin' he's been deservin' for a mighty long time. A mighty long time, I reckon."

Homer looked at the sheriff for a few moments and then beyond the porch into the dark pecan orchard, and the fields beyond that. He was a man transfixed on something. Maybe something inside that needed to get out, or maybe something outside that needed to get in.

"Homer, it's good to see you out here," Tony said, "but I don't know why you showed up after the party's over."

"I figured I might be able to help still. Even though y'all seem to have taken care of everything out here."

Homer had seen my car parked away from the cabin and drove on until he saw what had happened on the porch. Then he had pulled in.

"Well, maybe there's somethin' you could do for us," Tony said.

"Yes, sir. What do y'all need?"

"We got Clyde Ferrell tied up back there behind his trailer," Tony said. "You think you could get him and walk him up here? He won't cause you any problems. I promise you that. He'd probably rather see you than Lard."

"Glad to help. I'll go get 'im."

As Homer walked into the darkness and out of sight, Abby and I walked out of the cabin onto the porch. I saw the truck and thought first of Homer. I wasn't sure, but it looked like his.

"Who's here?" I said.

"More deputies," Tony said.

"What in the hell. . ."

"Kidding, John," Lard said. "Relax. It's Homer Jones. Tony sent him after Clyde."

"How'd he know? Why's he here?" I said.

"Damn if I know," Tony said, "but we'll ask him when he gets back."

Abby thanked Tony and Lard for putting themselves in danger to help her. She hugged them both and kissed them on their cheeks.

"If I'd known I'd get a kiss, we'd been here a lot sooner," Lard said.

"I owed them something too, Abby," Tony said. "They gave up on me and came after you. I'm glad you're safe, but this thing was about me, too."

"Good enough, Tony," Abby said. "It's all over now, I hope anyway."

"Well, we still got us a big problem here," Tony said, "and I hope everybody understands it."

"What's that?" I said.

"What're we gonna do about these fine lawmen now?" Tony said. "Sheriff runs this county. Hell, he runs this part of the state. Who do we turn to now?"

I looked around the porch, at the cabin and down at the sheriff and his deputy. Luther was still rubbing his head. Sheriff Dupree was looking into the night across the dirt road in front of the cabin. He had been staring that way and hadn't moved since a couple of minutes earlier when Lard had finally gotten off him.

"I'm going to call Mickey Burke, my editor," I said, "and explain this mess to him and maybe he can figure out what to do, who to call. He's not going to believe it, but he needs to hear it now. We need help."

"Another front-page story for Mr. Big Shot," Tony said, smiling, but keeping a steady hand on Luther's pistol.

"Not this way, Tony," I said. "Oh, hell, no, I never wanted to be there this way. Not what's happened to you and now Abby."

I walked back into the cabin and Abby followed. I picked up the telephone on an end table near the chair where Abby had been tied. I dialed the operator for Mickey's home phone number. I had not before that night called Mickey at home. He was having a gin and tonic and watching the Braves game. He answered after the first ring.

"Hello."

He answered in the same hard, barking voice he used the newsroom. That voice at that moment was both comforting and unmistakable.

"Mickey, this is John Maynard and I'm still up at the river. And. . .uh. . .well me and Abby have got a pretty big story up here and we need. . ."

"Damn, Maynard. I know you do. Why in the hell are you calling me at this hour and telling me this? I know you got a big story."

"No, Mickey. There's something more. A lot more."

Mickey listened, and I told the whole thing, beginning with where Abby was and what she was doing the moment they took her. I included Tony's statement that it was Luther Wright's car that ran him off the road, trying to kill him after the meeting at the Opry Barn. My story and facts were clear and concise and without unnecessary words. It only took me a couple of minutes, and before I stopped I asked Mickey what we should do with the three lawmen we were holding at Luther's cabin.

"Well, goddamnit Maynard, I told you weeks ago to stay on this thing, and I'll be damned if you didn't. I'm proud of you, goddamnit. And everybody's okay? Abby's okay? Right?"

"Scared Mickey. She was scared. We were both scared. We're okay, but what are we going to do now? We need help."

"You hang tight and I'll call the GBI. I got a contact there in Cordele, and he can get to you in a few minutes. You give me your phone number there, and if I need to I'll call you back. I'll have somebody there soon. Real soon."

I found the cabin's telephone number on top of the phone and told Mickey what it was.

"Thanks. We'll be waiting. We want to get out of here, Mickey. It's been a damn mess."

"I know you do. I'll make the call now. Hang tight, Maynard."

Mickey hung up and dialed the home of Hodge Hamilton, who worked for the Georgia Bureau of Investigation. Twenty minutes later three unmarked cars and nine agents pulled into Luther's driveway. At about the time Mickey made his call, Homer Jones walked Clyde from the trailer to the front porch. Clyde was rubbing his chin. He still felt Lard's fist.

When Hamilton and the agents got out of their cars, the sheriff and his two deputies were sitting on the porch, all three looking in different directions. Tony gave Luther's gun to Hodge Hamilton, who was the first to walk up the steps. He was glad to get rid of it.

"Which one of you is John Maynard?" Hamilton said.

Hamilton was wearing a black jacket with gold GBI lettering on the back, as were the other agents. The jackets covered the guns they were carrying.

"I'm John Maynard."

"Son, I need a statement from you and Ms. Sinclair. I won't take long tonight, but I'll need more later, probably tomorrow. You understand don't you?"

"Yes, sir. I understand."

Hamilton turned and spoke to Abby. "You're Ms. Sinclair?"

"Yes, but please call me Abby."

"Fine with me."

Abby, myself, and Hodge Hamilton walked into the cabin and sat at the white linoleum kitchen table where there were a few empty beer cans and a half-full fifth of Jack Daniels. Hamilton found a clean place to work and took out a long yellow paper notepad and a black pen. He asked questions of both of us and wrote what we said. He was thorough and so were we.

Tony, Lard, and Homer Jones were questioned by other agents on the front porch and as they spoke agents copied what they said. Fifteen minutes later the interviews ended. Abby and I, along with Agent Hamilton, returned to the front porch.

"We know everything that happened today," Hamilton said, "and when we get these three in front of the feds, they may tell us why. Kidnapping brings in the FBI, and I made the call before I left my house. They should be here soon."

"It's about this river and what that company's been doin' do it," Tony said. "That's what all this is about. They are connected with Transpower. What else could it be? Transpower has to be behind all this."

"We all know what it's about," Lard said. "Feed the monkey and watch 'im shit."

"You two may be right," Hamilton said, "but we'll see how it plays out. Whatever it is, we'll get to it eventually. I promise you that."

Hamilton looked at the three disgraced lawmen, who had kept silent during all of this, refusing to answer any questions until their lawyer was present.

"Mr. Hamilton, there's something that's been left out," Homer said. "No one asked about it, but it all needs to be said here tonight. Yes, sir, it does. I aim to say it."

"What's your name again?" Hamilton said.

He removed his pen again from his shirt pocket and found a clean page on his notepad.

"Homer Jones, sir. It was at my place where they took her. When they took Miss Abby."

Homer looked at Abby for the first time.

"Mr. Jones, what do you want to say to us about all of this?" Hamilton said. "What hasn't been said? I'm listening."

Homer told them of a conversation he had overhead a few weeks ago while he was taking a break from his grounds-keeping job at the Crisp County Courthouse. He was sitting on a bench under an oak tree when Luther and Clyde walked out of the sheriff's office on their way to their patrol car in the parking lot. That was not unusual, but what they were saying was.

"They didn't see me because of the big tree. Biggest one in the city. I heard what they said. Every word. I heard it all. Yes sir. I heard it all."

Homer then hesitated looking off into the night.

Hamilton waited a few seconds before he spoke.

"What was it? What did they say?"

"Big money, sir. Big money. It was Luther who said the hundred thousand dollars had gone to Sheriff Dupree from the company big shots after John Maynard's first newspaper story. Yes, sir. I heard every word."

"What story?" Hamilton said.

"The one with Tony talkin' bad about Transpower. It was the river story on the front page of the *Chronicle*. How the river was all messed up by the company. Yes, sir. Heard every word."

Hamilton kept writing. Tony and Lard said nothing. Neither did I.

"And then I heard something else, sir. There was something else I heard when the both of them were in the parking lot. I'll never forget it, sir."

"What was it?"

"Luther tells Clyde he'd get enough to buy a cabin," Homer said. "Just like his. Make sure there's no more stories in the paper and Clyde could get a cabin just like Luther's. No more Tony Patrick in the paper. Yes, sir. That's what he said. What Luther said. I heard every word."

"You telling me that the company paid Sheriff Dupree a hundred thousand dollars to shut Tony Patrick up?" Hamilton said. "To run him off the road and try to kill him? To kidnap a reporter. Is that what you're telling me?"

"No, sir, I am not. Didn't hear a word about killing Tony or kidnapping Miss Abby. No sir. Not one word. I'm telling you exactly what I heard that afternoon at the courthouse. I know what I heard, and I know what I see, and I'd swear on a Bible to what I heard that afternoon."

"But I believe that's what he's telling us," Tony said. "What else is the money for?"

"Why didn't you go to the police that day?" Hamilton said.

"I got my reasons and they are good ones," Homer said. "I told one person only. That was Willard Gentry. That's all. Just Willard."

Hamilton knew of Gentry, like most folks who spent any time around the river and lake. Everyone knew Willard Gentry.

"I was goin' to tell John Maynard in my house today until all of this happened. All this got in the way."

Homer looked at the cabin, then at Abby and down at the three lawmen who remained silent.

"Why Willard Gentry?" Hamilton said. "He's a good man, but not a police officer. Why'd you tell him?"

Then Homer Jones told us another story.

# CHAPTER 19

She was seventeen when it happened, and it happened at the End of the Line. Luther's cabin wasn't there all those years ago. There were other things that were different in the 1940s on this land, and among the black and white people who walked and worked on it. Things were much different then.

She had been picking cotton all day for Sonny Dupree's father, and when Melva finished working, her strong dark hands were bleeding. She didn't think much about that. It always ended that way. Over the last few weeks, she had been thinking about only one thing, and that was Homer and how much she loved him. She knew he loved her in the same way. She wanted to be with him forever, she said to herself a thousand times, and in every way a wife should be. She said it to him, too. Being with him in the bed for the first time made her nervous thinking about it. Her mother had told her nothing about those kinds of things. She loved him whole. That's all she knew. Everything else would be okay as long as she could be with Homer. They'd be happy together and make a good life the best they could. Have children and a house of their own. That's how she thought all day long with each cotton ball she picked and placed in the long sack tied to her waist. Bloody fingers at the end of the day.

Homer was working on another farm a couple of miles from the End of the Line. The Gentry family owned that land and planted cotton and peanuts and sometimes corn. Cattle and hogs were raised there. Homer had been a good worker for Willard Gentry Sr. over the last two years, and hoped to continue working for him after he and Melva married. He thought it to be a secure job for a long time. He'd live, work, and die on this land. Love Melva and make a family with her.

Homer, two years older than Melva, had not told anyone within or out of his family about what he and Melva were planning to do. It made him anxious to think about it. Soon he would have to tell them all what they were planning. It had been decided and he could wait no longer.

Willard Gentry Jr. was Homer's age, and the two worked alongside each other and sometimes afterwards in the spring and summer went swimming together in the Flint River. When the nights were cool, they'd make a fire and cook fresh catfish caught on trotlines they set across the river and along its banks. They laughed and told stories and had fun together. Never once talked about what it meant to be black or white in a white man's world. Never once.

Melva Jackson was proud of the two dollars she earned that day for twelve hours of picking, and was walking the half mile home to give the money to her father to help the family. She would keep a quarter for herself. She had five brothers and two sisters and her momma and daddy needed her help. Everybody picked. Everybody worked. She had thought about Homer all day and how bad she wanted to marry him and love him, but was scared, knowing soon she was going to have to tell her parents. It had to be real soon, Homer said.

"We need to tell all them real soon, Melva. They all got to know."

He had proposed marriage to her and she had accepted. What would her momma and daddy say? Girls her age got married all the time. That's what Homer said.

A moment before she saw the headlights of a truck and heard the laughter and loud voices coming from it along the End of the Line, she felt a cool breeze run across her face and for a few seconds the day's hard work had been forgotten. The calm evening sky in its orange glow, and the constant thought of her love for Homer, was a reprieve from the cotton fields. She looked up at the fading sun and closed her eyes and thought about loving Homer.

Then the truck raced by her and after about fifty yards it stopped kicking up dust from the End of the Line. When she saw the truck stop, her stomach turned over.

"Goddamnit, I told you sorry asses to stop back there!" Sonny Dupree said. "There's something I been meanin' to do for a long time. Now's a good time to do it."

Sonny was the same age as Homer. He took another drink from the whiskey bottle and threw it into the row of pine trees along where he and his three buddies had stopped. Sonny was riding in the back of the truck when he saw Melva.

"Well, goddamn you, I didn't hear you," the driver said. He didn't turn around to look at Sonny. He was drinking whiskey, too.

With the truck stopped, Sonny jumped out and began walking toward Melva. Steady, quick steps.

"You sumbitches wait right here" Sonny said. "You can look but don't touch. Don't even get close. I ain't sharin' with anyone. This one is all mine. Won't take me long."

He began to walk faster toward her. She stopped on the side of the road as he was coming. Melva began to shake. Even before he got to her, she could smell the bitter whiskey. She could smell the hatred. She thought about running, but didn't. She stood still, her body tired and her mind now overcome with fear.

"That's right, my little black bitch-baby," Sonny said. "You ain't goin' nowhere now. You're all mine, purty black bitch. You just a purty black bitch."

"Mr. Dupree, sir, Mr. Dupree, I'm just going home. I bin pickin' cotton for your daddy. Just like always. Done worked hard today. All day long. Just like always. I worked hard all day for your daddy."

Her sentences were ended when Sonny's right fist hit her under her jaw, and her body tumbled over, rolling off the road into the ditch that carried rainwater into the Flint River. She lay there motionless.

Sonny ripped from her the tattered brown dress her mother had made for her from a gunnysack. She didn't move or cry out when he was doing the awful thing to her. His fingernails clawed into her face leaving streaks of red down her cheeks. He ravaged her as if he wanted to claw her eyes out. Still she said nothing. If she had struggled, he would've beat her over the head and maybe killed her. He pushed her legs apart. She was about to cry out when he entered her, but she didn't. He hurt her, and the pain swelled up in her body like nothing she had experienced before that day. It was over in a couple of minutes, just like he said it would be. But the thing he did to her would last forever.

"Now my little purty black bitch, you can go home to your mommy and daddy and tell 'em it was a good fuck," Sonny said. "Tell 'em we had us a real good fuck. You like it just like the others."

He turned away from her and walked back to the truck and his drunken friends.

In Melva's right hand she had held on to the two dollars she had earned that day. Through the whole time she was being raped, she never let it go. She didn't move until she could not longer hear the truck and when she did, she hurt everywhere.

Blood was streaking down her right thigh. When she saw the blood, she began to cry in loud wailing sounds as if the end of the world was near. The crying went that way until she became too exhausted to continue. She tried to stand, but couldn't.

Then she heard the truck again. It was coming to her. She said to herself, "No matter what they do to me, I won't let them see me cry when they doin' it. I got to be strong like my daddy says. I'll be strong."

She waited. The truck stopped. It was almost dark now.

"Are you hurt? What's wrong with ya?" the driver said.

The driver turned the engine off and got out of the truck. Here it comes again, she thought. Here it comes. She was still lying in the ditch.

Then Melva recognized the voice of Willard Gentry. She had been around him a few times when he and Homer had been together. She had liked Willard, and Homer had said he and his family were "mostly good white folks that we could trust a little." Willard had been polite to her and talked to her and treated her like he would a white person. She thought it odd. It was his voice she heard from above.

"Mr. Gentry, I hurt so bad. Please don't tell Homer what they done did to me. Please don't tell my momma and daddy."

She cried in full again and in long wailing sounds. It took a couple of minutes before she was able to stop.

"Oh, Melva, what've they done to you?" Willard said. "What have they done to you, Melva? Who did this?"

"They broke me all up," Melva said. "All up in the inside. I hurt everywhere." Melva rolled over with her face to the ground.

"I'll help you up," Willard said. "Don't let me hurt you. I'm going to get you to a doctor, Melva. You need help."

He slid both of his arms under her and raised her from the ground. She made not a sound. He carried her to his truck bed, and laid her on top of a pile of empty gunnysacks. Homer had helped him empty the sacks of feed corn earlier that day.

Willard got back into his truck and drove her into Cordele to Dr. Willis Inman's house. Inman had grown up with Willard's father and was the only white doctor Willard knew who would treat blacks. Willard stopped in front of Inman's house, picked up Melva again and carried her to the front door. He knocked on the door. The doctor answered and Willard carried her inside and placed her on the doctor's sofa. The doctor took over then.

Next Willard drove to Homer Jones' home, picked him up and took him into Cordele to Dr. Inman's house. Willard told Homer what he had done for Melva, and what he believed had happened to her. Homer stared out the truck window and said nothing as they drove to Cordele. A few moments later, he raised both hands, covered his face, and wept. Willard stopped the truck in front of the doctor's house, they got out and went in together.

The baby boy came two months early and lived three hours and died. Melva had not chosen a name, but held the child in her arms before he died. Afterwards Melva's crying kept coming for days. Her body would fully recover but other parts of her would not. They never would.

It was at this point in the story on the front porch of Luther's cabin when Homer stopped the telling, and looked away from us. The pause lasted a few moments as he turned away from the porch with his back to us and looked to the distance, toward the End of the Line. Then he turned toward us again and continued.

"Melva and me got married a few months after that child of Dupree's was born and died. And what that man did to my Melva was done to others we knew. Everybody then was afraid to say anything. Afraid we'd all be kilt. That was the old days."

Homer said he worked on the Gentry farm for several years and they were good and decent folks. He maintained a friendship with Willard Gentry Jr. as they both grew into manhood, married, and had children of their own. They never forgot the old days.

"When Melva was dying with cancer and needed treatment, it was Willard Gentry who drove us to Atlanta," Homer said. "He even gave us money when things got tight. I always paid him back. Always did."

"That's why he was the only one you told about the conversation you overheard at the courthouse?" GBI agent Hamilton said. "The conversation about the hundred thousand dollars?"

"Yes, sir," Homer said. "That'd be true. I could always trust Mr. Willard Gentry. Still do. Could always trust him. Trusted him back in the old days."

"Did he ever tell you to go to the police?" Hamilton said. "To the GBI?"

"Yes, sir, he did. I wasn't ready to do it. I didn't want nothin' to do with any policeman. Anytime, anywhere. I still 'member the old days, Mr. Hamilton. They hard to forget. But Mr. Willard told me if I ain't goin' tell the police, I should tell this here reporter. Mr. John Maynard. That's what he told me. You see Willard told me to be on the lookout for this newspaper reporter. This one here."

"So you weren't surprised to see Mr. Maynard today at your house?" Hamilton said.

"No sir. I figured it wouldn't be much longer before Mr. Willard directed him to me. He told he was goin' to do it. When the girl came up missin', well, I figured right by comin' out here. I figured right all right."

"Were you planning to tell John Maynard everything you've told us tonight?" Hamilton said. "Was that your plan?"

"I 'spect I was. Willard said this reporter was an honest young man tryin' to do somethin' good. I believed Willard. Besides, you just never know what's caught on your trotline 'til you pull it up. All the way up."

I looked at Homer and though the sadness relived through Melva's story was painful to him, he smiled just the same.

# Chapter 20

Three weeks after the night at Luther's cabin, I wrote another in a series of stories about what happened that hot summer along the Flint River and Lake Blackshear. This was part of the story on page one, above the fold:

> MACON – Crisp County Sheriff Sonny Dupree and two of his deputies, Luther Wright and Clyde Ferrell, all pleaded guilty yesterday in federal court to charges of kidnapping and bribery in connection with an *Albany Chronicle* reporter and Transpower Inc.
>
> Dupree, a former Georgia Lawman of the Year, and his deputies could each face up to twenty years in prison. They will be sentenced next week...

The story detailed the hundred thousand dollars promised to Sheriff Dupree from Transpower to "shut Tony Patrick up." I used that quote in the third paragraph, and it was attributed to Dupree's confession based on the GBI's investigation.

A few weeks later, I wrote another story about the guilty pleas from both the plant manager and public relations officer at the Transpower plant outside of Cordele. They were charged with bribery, conspiracy, and other charges and could face up to twenty years in prison as well. Sentencing for them was scheduled for one month later.

By the end of September 1983, company big shots from their corporate headquarters in Akron, Ohio, had flown their private jet to the Albany Municipal Airport to conduct a press conference. I was covering the story, and Abby was assigned to photograph the executives apologizing for the criminal activity of two of their employees.

Abby wore a big straw hat with a green and orange flowery band that I had bought for her at the Gator Pit. It protected her well from the sun that day. She looked good in it.

The executives announced that the company was going to spend ten million dollars to construct and maintain holding ponds that would allow their pulp wood waste to settle before discharging it into the river. They promised the Flint River and Lake Blackshear would return to normal conditions within a year.

No more dead animals. No more putrid water. Tony Patrick had been fighting for this all along, and it was a fight that almost killed him and could've done the same to Abby.

The biologist I interviewed following that press conference said this would have a "dramatic and positive impact on the river's water quality." I used the quote in the lede.

I was at my desk the morning the story appeared committing the company to cleaning up its mess, when Mickey Burke walked over and sat down next to me.

"Maynard, I'm proud of you, goddamnit. You and Abby both. You two put yourselves out there in a helluva of a lot of danger for the newspaper and the public. You stayed with it and got those bastards in the end. The paper's proud of you. I'm proud of you. Hell, the whole state should be proud of you."

"Thanks, Mickey. I just fell into it, I guess. And Abby was a big help. I appreciate all your support. It was hard at times."

"It was a damn fine piece of newspaper work. Both of you working together like that. Damn good work, Maynard. Here's something I want you two to share."

He pulled an envelope out of his jacket and placed it on my desk next to my black Royal typewriter. I picked the envelope up, opened it, and pulled something out. It was a check from the *Chronicle* for two thousand dollars.

"Mickey, what's this for?" I said.

"It's for you and Abby. Take a few weeks off and go have some fun together. You deserve it. Both of you do. It's made out to both of you."

"I appreciate this and Abby will too."

"Have some fun and just let me know when you two are going to be out. Lots of work to do when you get back."

He got up and walked back to his desk. About half way to his desk, Mickey stopped and turned around.

"When you get back, we're going to move Abby down to the newsroom with us full-time. You can tell her first if you want to, and then I'll talk to her about it later."

"She'll be excited. I do know that."

I picked up the telephone and called Abby who was upstairs in the features section writing a story about a woman who ran a nursery and made straw hats for the children in the shapes of animals. She picked up the telephone.

"Abby Sinclair, *Albany Chronicle.*"

"Hey, it's me."

"Hey, it's me too, Johnny Boy. It's still me for you."

"I got something to tell you. Something you'll like to hear."

"Oh, no, we're going back to the river. Is that it Johnny Boy? Is that what you're going to tell me? We got another assignment on the river?"

"It could be. But it might be a different river. Maybe the River Liffy in Ireland. If that's what you want."

"What do you mean by that?"

"Here's what I mean. I'm holding a check for two thousand dollars that Mickey gave us to have some fun. He says take a couple weeks off. He says we deserve it. And I agree. But that's not all."

"There's more? What could be better than what you just told me?"

"When we come back, you'll be down in the newsroom full-time. He's going to work it all out with your department up there. How about that?"

"John, that's great news to me. Both parts."

"We ought to go somewhere for a couple of weeks. Where should we go? You got any suggestions?"

"I'm with you, Johnny Boy. Wherever you want."

"France, Ireland, maybe we'll visit Van Morrison and Yeats. Maybe Rimbaud or James Joyce. I know some of these guys have been dead for a few years, but if we look hard, we'll see them anyway. I promise you we can find them."

"Oh, I can't wait. The countryside and poetry in Ireland. You think we can do it?"

"Not without conditions."

"You just name it, Johnny Boy. Any condition you want."

"Okay, I'll name it. There's only one condition. If you stop to look at tomato plants or anything that reminds you of your mother, or just *anything*, I won't leave you and you won't leave me. Got to promise me that, Abby."

"It's a promise, Johnny Boy."

## AUTHOR'S NOTE

This is a work of fiction based on actual events in South Georgia in the early 1980s. Thanks to my editor, Rosemary Barnes of Atlanta, for finding many ways to make my manuscript better. And thanks to my niece, Anna Cone of Baltimore who produced the mysterious and compelling cover art. I love it.

## ABOUT THE AUTHOR

After five non-fiction books, this is my first work of fiction and my hope is there will be others. Before I began my teaching career in the late 1980s, I worked for a handful of newspapers in the Southeast, including the *Albany (GA) Herald*. I live in Fayetteville, GA, with my wife Phyllis and teach at Fayette County High School.

My books are available at www.amazon.com

Made in the USA
Coppell, TX
24 September 2020

38726704R00111